ASKING
FOR IT

INSATIABLE
by Sherri L. King, Elizabeth Jewell & S. L. Carpenter

HIS FANTASIES, HER DREAMS
by Sherri L. King, S. L. Carpenter & Trista Ann Michaels

MASTER OF SECRET DESIRES
by S. L. Carpenter, Elizabeth Jewell & Tawny Taylor

BEDTIME, PLAYTIME
by Jaid Black, Sherri L. King & Ruth D. Kerce

HURTS SO GOOD
by Gail Faulkner, Lisa Renee Jones & Sahara Kelly

LOVER FROM ANOTHER WORLD
by Rachel Carrington, Elizabeth Jewell & Shiloh Walker

FEVER-HOT DREAMS
by Sherri L. King, Jaci Burton & Samantha Winston

TAMING HIM
by Kimberly Dean, Summer Devon & Michelle M. Pillow

ALL SHE WANTS
by Jaid Black, Dominique Adair & Shiloh Walker

ASKING FOR IT

KIT TUNSTALL

JOANNA WYLDE

ELISA ADAMS

POCKET BOOKS

New York   London   Toronto   Sydney

Pocket Books
A Division of Simon & Schuster, Inc.
1230 Avenue of the Americas
New York, NY 10020

First Pocket Books trade paperback edition September 2008

ISBN-13: 978-1-4165-7761-4
ISBN-10:   1-4165-7761-0

CONTENTS

ABLAZE
KIT TUNSTALL
1

BE CAREFUL WHAT YOU WISH FOR
JOANNA WYLDE
63

DROP DEAD SEXY
ELISA ADAMS
189

ABLAZE

KIT TUNSTALL

ONE

BLACK SMOKE BILLOWED DOWN the hallway, obscuring Nick's view through his face shield. His peripheral vision tracked two teenagers in the Westbridge Academy's conservative uniforms hurrying toward the exit, clutching hands and sobbing. He thought about stopping the girls to ask if they had seen anyone else left in the building, but the air of panic surrounding them indicated they wouldn't be responsive.

Seeing they required no assistance, he and his partner moved on, Paula taking the lead. As they progressed down the hallway, the smoke thickened, settling lower to the floor. He reached for his SCBA automatically as they checked each classroom, quickly but methodically.

At the last room in the hallway, where the fire had originated, Nick and Paula stepped inside, dropping to a crouch as they moved through the room, searching for anyone remaining. His low vantage point allowed him to avoid the thickest concentration of the acrid smoke and improved his visibility.

The room appeared to be a science lab containing several long black tables with three chairs at each. All of the tables were bare of the clutter of academic paraphernalia, indicating either everyone had grabbed their belongings, or no one had been in the room when the fire started.

Under that assumption, he didn't expect to find anyone but indicated with a hand signal to Paula that he was checking the adjoining lab, as procedure dictated. With Paula behind him, he entered the second room, and his heart stuttered when he saw someone lying facedown on the floor in the corner. Nick moved closer at a rapid pace, identifying the form of a woman when he knelt beside her. As Paula joined him, he rolled the woman onto her back and lifted her in his arms, not taking time to check her vitals. She settled over his shoulder easily. The woman was a negligent burden on his way from the building, and he emerged into fresh air seconds later, his partner close on his heels. Paula broke off to rejoin the group of firefighters gathered round the engine.

Nick went straight to one of the ambulances, where an EMT waited to care for her. He lowered the woman onto a waiting stretcher and stripped off his SCBA then pushed back his face shield, preparing to find his chief to inform him the building was clear. Nick's eyes fell on the face of the woman, and he caught his breath. Even the black smudges couldn't disguise her finely honed features. With olive skin and dark brown hair, she was a striking contrast to the crisp white sheet and pillow on the gurney.

Her eyes opened as the EMT slipped an oxygen mask over her face. The rich brown color reminded Nick of pools of molten chocolate. The bewilderment in them made his heart ache. Without removing his elkskin gloves, he took her hand and squeezed gently. "Everything's going to be fine, ma'am."

For a long second, her gaze didn't waver from his. Nick had the sensation she was peering into his soul. He squirmed at the thought, breaking eye contact when he caught sight of the chief. It was a struggle to release the woman's hand, much to his surprise.

Glancing down once more, he saw her eyes had closed again. The sound of her harsh coughing remained with him as he made his way to Brady, the chief. Her frightened eyes haunted him, and it took all his willpower to push away thoughts of her and return to the business at hand. Never had he experienced such a connection in such a way, and the woman's image stayed with him as he rejoined the rest of the crew extinguishing the fire.

BREATHING HURT. COUGHING HURT even more, but Miri couldn't stifle the urge. The oxygen provided some relief from the burning, acrid sensation in her throat and lungs but didn't repress the reflex to clear the congestion. She was vaguely aware of the EMT hovering beside her, monitoring her vitals every few minutes, but couldn't manage to converse yet. Her throat was too raw. Even the thought of speaking made her wince.

The approach of a firefighter, stripped of his Nomex jacket, with a white T-shirt and red Nomex pants, distracted her temporarily from her misery. Miri's eyes widened when she recognized the black-haired, blue-eyed hunk as the man who had carried her from the building. Her stomach clenched with nerves—or the urge to vomit after a prolonged coughing fit—as he approached, a smile displaying his firm lips, set in a tanned face, to their best advantage.

He tapped the EMT on the arm. "How's she doing, Manny?"

"Pretty well." He pointed to the pulse oximeter attached to Miri's finger. "Her oxygen is ninety-eight."

"Will you be taking her to the hospital?"

Miri moved the oxygen mask. "No." She hardly recognized the hoarse voice emerging from her throat.

He turned his attention to her. "How're you feeling, ma'am?"

"Thirsty."

"I can take care of that."

She watched him walk away from her, heading toward the red engine with PHFD emblazoned on the side in black letters. The loose fit of his pants hid his buttocks and legs, but the T-shirt clung to his defined arms like a lover, revealing each bulge and flex.

When he returned, water bottle in hand, Miri quickly dropped her eyes to hide the fact she had been staring. The instant attraction to her rescuer disturbed her. She wasn't the type to have her head turned so quickly, and definitely not just by physical attributes. She tried telling herself gratitude was the only thing she felt for the man, but knew it wasn't true.

"Here you are, Ms.—" He unscrewed the cap before handing her the bottle.

"Zorga. Miriam Zorga." She handed the mask to Manny, nodding to acknowledge his cautionary words of sipping slowly, and took a small taste. The water was like Heaven, though tainted by the flavor of smoke lingering in her mouth. After two more small sips, she looked up at the firefighter. "Thank you for the water . . . and for saving my life."

He inclined his head. "That's my job."

"Still, I want to repay you. May I buy you dinner Friday night?" Miri's eyes widened at the invitation. What was she thinking? She never dated a man unless she had known him for a decent length of time, knew his character, friends, interests and flaws. She did not go out with men she had just met, no matter how sexy. She certainly wasn't the one to issue the request. A retraction hovered on the tip of her tongue, but his reply cut it off.

"It's not every day a beautiful woman offers me dinner. How can I say no?" His blue eyes sparkled, as if he sensed she had been about to withdraw the invitation.

She couldn't graciously change her mind now. Miri forced a small smile. "Does Poplin Hills Country Club suit you?"

"If that's what you want." The idea didn't seem to thrill him. "I'll pick you up if you'll give me your address."

"No." She winced at the panic in her tone, hoping the lingering huskiness masked it. "We'll meet there. Seven thirty?" She held her breath, expecting him to argue. Hoping he would, giving her an out from the evening. She wouldn't feel at all guilty for rescinding the invitation should he prove to be forceful or controlling. To her disappointment, he simply nodded.

"I'll see you then." He started to turn but paused, looking down at her. "I'm Nick Martin, by the way." Then he was gone, fading back into the chaos of the scene on the front lawn of the staid private girls' school.

She blushed upon realizing she hadn't even caught his name before asking him to dinner. Hormones were to blame for her spontaneous action, which alarmed her further. She hadn't surrendered to the pull of hormones as a teenager. *It's about time you did*, whispered a sly voice in her mind—the voice she was careful to always repress and tune out. This time, it refused to be ignored, whispering all sorts of erotic suggestions about how the dinner date with Nick might end. Much to her surprise, she didn't want to ignore the voice this time.

MIRI GROANED AT THE sight in the mirror. Her attempt at sexy had ended up closer to disheveled. Thick hair hung around her face in a tangled mass, refusing to lie sleek, as she had envisioned. The black silk pants she hadn't worn for years reminded her why she hadn't worn them with the way they clung to her thighs, accentuating the cellulite she hid under skirts and looser slacks. The red shirt dipped too low, exposing what should have been generous cleavage on a different woman, but merely accented what she lacked.

Miri glanced at the clock, biting her lip. She had twenty minutes until she was supposed to meet Nick. Availing herself of valet parking would give her five extra minutes to fix the disastrous sight she currently presented. In record time, she stripped off the slacks and shirt, and standing before the mirror in plain beige panties and a simple bra, she grabbed her hair and pulled it back. Her hands were adept at forming the bun she wore every day, so that took little time. She secured it with pins and turned to her wardrobe, once again examining her available clothing. Everything seemed wrong, which had already led her to the two sexiest pieces she owned, and look how they had turned out.

With a sigh, she selected an A-line brown skirt and camel turtleneck sweater with subtle threads of gold woven throughout. Adding gold hoops and a pearl necklace made the outfit dressy enough for the country club, though boring. She chose to look on the bright side as she scooped up a gold clutch and hurried from her small house. Boring was sure to be a turnoff to the all-male Nick Martin, who must be accustomed to dating beautiful women. If he had no interest in her, that saved her the effort of fighting her attraction to him. The thought provided little consolation as she pushed her beige Saab four miles over the speed limit through the sparsely populated streets of Poplin Hills.

SHE ARRIVED FIVE MINUTES late, to find Nick sitting at the bar, watching for her. She nodded to the maitre d' on her way through the spacious entryway, sparing no time to admire the antique teak, gold accents and deep red carpeting. The surroundings were familiar to her.

As she approached, Nick eased off his bar stool, drink in hand.

He tugged at the tie around his neck, as if unaccustomed to such accoutrements. With a critical eye, Miri examined him, noting he was sexy in the black suit but obviously uncomfortable. Her choice of restaurants was clearly a failure.

"I'm so sorry I'm not on time," she said in a rush when reaching him. "I'm never late . . . " She trailed off, deciding not to elaborate on why she was tardy.

He shrugged. "Don't worry. The beer is cold, and this is a nice place to wait." His expression betrayed the small white lie. Miri bit back a gasp at the electricity flaring between them when he took her hand. "All that matters is you showed up."

She cleared her throat, resisting the urge to tug her hand from his. The contact discomfited her. Not because he was a stranger, but because she liked it too much. "Are you ready for dinner?"

He nodded as the maitre d' appeared at their side, as if psychically summoned. Nick didn't release her hand while they followed the man to a round table draped with a red tablecloth. Gold candleholders shone in the muted illumination from the crystal chandelier above the table. The flames from the red candles provided a cozy glow to accentuate the overhead lighting.

She breathed a sigh of relief when he had to let go of her hand as she prepared to sit at the table. The light-headedness his touch had inspired almost faded, though she still felt giddy. Inner alarms screamed warnings about his effect on her, but Miri tried to ignore them as Nick pulled out her chair and seated her. Once again, his touch made her breathless.

Awkward silence fell between them as the maitre d' departed after promising their server's attention shortly. She stared across the table, struggling not to stare into his sinfully blue eyes while trying to avoid the appearance of rudeness by ducking his gaze. She couldn't strike a balance and ended up looking away.

"Do you come here often?" His mood was difficult to discern. He didn't seem nervous, merely out of his element. Nick's voice didn't betray anything other than mild curiosity.

She nodded. "I have a lifetime membership." Miri didn't share the complete history of how it came to her. Her mother's numerous sordid marriages weren't a topic for first-date discussion. "It was a gift from my stepfather. He owned Poplin Hills Country Club a few years ago." Stepfather number four, to be precise, and the only one she had ever loved as a father.

His brow furrowed. "Richard Grazier was your stepfather?"

She nodded, struggling to maintain an indifferent façade as she studied him subtly, searching for a hint of avarice. More than once, she had disappointed a suitor who thought her stepfather had left her a large inheritance. His death had been several years after the divorce, and Miri had refused to accept anything from him other than companionship at that point. His other children and current wife had been relieved.

"It was hard on the town when Mr. Grazier passed. Everyone loved him."

Her heart softened at his sympathetic tone, and she struggled to make an intelligent response while hiding the tears in her voice. Thankfully, the arrival of the waiter prevented a reply, allowing her a minute to compose herself as Nick ordered a steak. Her order of grilled tilapia came automatically, and the server moved away.

The sommelier arrived within seconds, handing the wine menu to Nick. "What will you have this evening, sir?"

Miri almost grinned at his deer-in-the-headlights look. It was clear he wasn't a wine aficionado. Smothering her mirth, she said, "I don't believe we'll need a bottle tonight, Jules. Would you please bring me a glass of sauvignon blanc?"

Jules turned to Nick. "For you, sir?"

"Beer's fine." Nick seemed unbothered by the wrinkling of the sommelier's brow as he left the table.

Again, the conversation lapsed. Miri asked a few meaning-less questions, as did he, while accomplishing nothing but killing time. Out of desperation, she asked about his family. That was a topic she rarely broached with a stranger, for fear of having to give reciprocal information, but something needed to move along their exchange.

His posture relaxed, and he began telling her about his large family, all currently living in Boston.

As Nick spoke of his relations, Miri tried not to let envy plague her. As she laughed along with him at his shared remembrances, she couldn't help contrasting his childhood to hers. Nick's had been full of family and love, while hers was one long stretch of loneliness, with no siblings to share the trauma of uncles and step-fathers constantly coming and going, and a mother who was more concerned about her sex life than her daughter's welfare.

As their meal arrived, she asked, "Why are you in Oregon if your family is in Boston?"

"I wanted to see something besides Boston. I ended up here after traveling a few years." He shook his head. "It's funny. I thought I wanted to break away from the family traditions, but I ended up a firefighter just like my brothers and father, in spite of myself. It just took me a few years longer."

Her eyes widened. "Everyone in your family is a firefighter?"

"Just about." Pride shone in his eyes. Before she could ask any-thing else, his expression dimmed. "My oldest brother isn't a fire-fighter now. He married a woman who hated the whole idea, so he gave it up." It was clear what Nick would do in a similar situa-tion. Miri would hate to be the woman to ask him to give up his career.

As they ate, they managed to fill the meal with stilted, meaningless conversation. By dessert, Miri had chalked up the date as a disaster and was admonishing herself about rash behavior when the bill arrived.

After settling the check, Miri rose to her feet, not waiting for Nick to pull out her chair. He rose just after her, putting his hand on her lower back as they left the restaurant. She searched for a painless way to close the evening while getting across the point that she didn't want a repeat. It probably wasn't a concern. What man would want a second date with her after this calamity?

Outside, she handed a slip to the valet, noticing Nick didn't. They stood in silence as the young woman brought forth her Saab. At the curb, Miri turned to him, extending her hand. "Thank you for allowing me to repay you for saving me, Nick."

His lips twitched, as if repressing laughter. "My pleasure, Miri." He took her hand, caressing the palm with small circles of his thumb.

With a decisive nod, she pulled her hand from his and slid inside through the opened car door. Miri looked up at him, trying not to let her eagerness to escape show. "Well . . . good night."

He nodded but made no effort to walk toward his own car, wherever it might be. She waited for him to speak or move, so she could close the door and drive away, but he just stood there. "Good night," she said again, allowing a hint of exasperation to show.

"I'll follow you home to make sure you get there safely."

"There's no need—"

He tapped on her windshield, already setting off in the direction of the self-parking area. "I'll catch up with you," he called over his shoulder.

She gritted her teeth and resisted the urge to run over him as he stepped in front of her car. No, she didn't want to dent the pristine grill, and blood would never come out of the beige paint.

As he jogged away, she slammed the door and shifted into drive, hitting the accelerator with a vengeance. All the way to her quiet home, she seethed with anger at his high-handedness. If he was pulling this stunt to get her to invite him in, he was in for a disappointment. Yes, he was too sexy for words, but she didn't like his attitude. He was too blunt for her tastes. She had cultivated a sophisticated life, courtesy of the time she had spent as Richard's stepdaughter. Nick would never fit into her existence. She couldn't even imagine him in her immaculate brick home, decorated in neutral colors with pastel accents.

She squirmed as an unwanted mental image came to her of Nick sprawled across her periwinkle Egyptian-cotton sheets with his hair tousled, his chest gleaming with sweat and the flush of passion still in his cheeks. Okay, there was one place he would complement her décor, but she refused to let her self-control slip enough to allow him into her home, much less the bedroom.

TWO

B Y THE TIME MIRI parked in her garage, Nick's red Dodge Ram had caught up with her. He stopped at her curb and bounded out without invitation to meet her at the door leading into the kitchen.

She pasted on a cool smile, valiantly ignoring the pool of heat that formed in her stomach when he touched her arm. "Thank you for the escort. It was unnecessary but appreciated."

He chuckled. "You don't lie well, Miri."

A blush swept through her cheeks. "Pardon?"

"You don't appreciate my chivalry. You're too busy trying to figure out what my angle is." He lifted an arm, resting his palm on the door behind her and bringing himself much closer.

Her spine stiffened. "You're mistaken, Mr. Martin. If you'll excuse me, I'm tired."

"Liar." His breath brushed her cheek. "You're thrumming with need. How long has it been since a man touched you here . . . " He brushed a hand across her hip. "Or here . . . " His hand moved higher to cup her stomach before inching up to just below her breast. "Or here?"

Breathlessness made it difficult to speak. "I . . . I'll scream . . . "

"No, you won't, because you want this. You wanted it from the moment you saw me." Nick leaned closer still, his lips brushing against her cheek. "Want to know how I know?"

She thought she shook her head but couldn't be certain. Every nerve in her body responded to his touch, and her brain couldn't seem to coordinate movements.

"It was the same for me." His voice lowered an octave. "From the moment I looked into your eyes, it was like a fist in the gut. I've thought about you all week."

Miri summoned a reserve of mental clarity. "I haven't thought about you at all. I want you to go now, or I'll have to call the police."

He ignored her, leaning closer still, almost touching her lips with his. "You want me. Why fight it?"

"How can I want you after that disaster of a date? We have nothing in common." She chewed her lower lip, finding it difficult to concentrate with his proximity. "We could never have anything besides a physical connection."

"We have sex in common. Why does it have to be more complicated than that?" He kissed her then, just for a second, but it was long enough to melt her insides. "I don't want a relationship. I saw what love did to my brother. That's the last thing I want."

Finally, they had something other than the physical in common. "I don't want to fall in love either." After seeing the way her mother moved from lover to lover so casually, Miri had decided at a young age she would rather be alone than have a string of affairs. She had maintained her resolve to avoid relationships, never meeting a man worth compromising for.

But it had been so long since a man had held her. Her last lover had been a memory for three years now, cast aside because he wanted a deeper emotional commitment than she would give.

"Great. We know what we want from this. What's the harm?"

She shivered at his breath against her lips. "I don't have one-night stands."

"How about two nights . . . or a week?" His husky laugh danced along her nerve endings, exciting them to a fever pitch. "Take it one day at a time, and we'll move on when we're no longer hot for each other."

She stared into his eyes, swimming in the molten desire reflected there. Her brain said no, but her body softened against his, and Miri licked her lips. She cursed her weakness, even as she put a hand on his chest. "Do you want to come in?"

HE SWALLOWED UP THE space inside her home. *Feng shui* had failed in this instance.

"You really like beige, don't you?"

Her neutral color scheme suddenly seemed boring next to Nick, and she had to resist the urge to hide the pastel pillows spread over the beige sofa. She owed him no excuses for her tasteful home, she reminded herself. "It's elegant."

Nick shrugged, dismissing the topic. "Coffee?"

She exhaled a breath she hadn't been aware of holding. It had been so long since a man had violated her sanctuary that she had forgotten how the process worked. Had she expected him to leap on her, take her on the floor and leave? Miri shook her head at the thought, squashing the ripple in the back of her mind that liked the scenario. "Of course. I have Seattle Sunrise or Mocha Mulberry."

His brow quirked. "Never mind. I'm strictly black, plain."

"Your loss. May I offer you an iced tea?"

Nick scanned her apartment. "Do you have beer?"

She shook her head. "I rarely drink at home."

"Tea is fine."

She turned to the kitchen, leaving Nick to settle on the sofa. As she peered through the opened top of the Dutch door, she saw him tossing her cushions haphazardly in the corner. Miri gritted her teeth to avoid saying something. She wasn't fitting the man into her life. Simply her bed.

Her hands shook at the thought, and she slopped a bit of tea from the pitcher onto the floor when removing it from the fridge. With a smothered curse, she ripped a paper towel from the roll on the counter and cleaned up the spot.

The dispenser on the refrigerator hummed, but no ice dropped into the glass when she pressed it against the sensor pad. Frowning, she bent at the waist to examine the dispenser just as the ice burst free, exploding from the chute into the glass, on the floor and at Miri.

She slammed the glass onto the counter with more force than necessary and bent to pick up the cubes. How many more signs did she need to know this was a bad idea? What had she been thinking, agreeing to a fling with Nick Martin, a man she had known less than a week? She couldn't allow libido to overrule common sense. Once he had his tea, she would explain she had changed her mind and send him away.

With that decision made, Miri's hands steadied, and she was able to get another glass, fill it with ice and put it on the counter. Not a drop of tea spilled from the pitcher as she filled the glasses, and she grasped them firmly before returning to the living room.

Nick hadn't waited for an invitation to make himself comfortable. He'd kicked off his shoes, removed his jacket and tie and rolled up the sleeves of his light blue shirt. His sock-covered feet screamed at her from their perch on her antique coffee table. She stared at them when putting his glass of tea on a coordinating coaster.

"Thanks." He patted the cushion beside him. "Sit with me."

She eyed the recliner and sat beside him with a soft sigh. Had he read her intentions to maintain distance between them?

Nick took the glass and gulped the tea in three long swallows. Miri watched his throat move, mesmerized by the cords flexing. Her mouth watered as she imagined trailing her tongue across his flesh.

To distract herself, she took a sip of tea and choked on it. Nick came to the rescue by patting her back, managing to knock the rest of the tea down the front of her sweater. She gasped as liquid soaked her front and then gasped again when Nick's bare hands brushed down her breasts in an effort to remove the ice cubes. She surrendered the glass to him, unable to speak for a moment.

"Come on. You need to get out of that. It's soaking wet." He took her hand, and Miri stood when he did and followed him down the hall. "Which room?"

She opened her mouth to tell him he had done enough, that he should leave now, but a small, "The door at the end of the hall," issued from her. What? Why was she so timid, going along with this? She wasn't that horny, was she?

Her nipples hardened at that moment as heat pooled between her thighs when she ran into Nick's back. Her body reeled from the contact, forcing her mind to admit maybe she was that turned on. She wanted him more than any man who had ever been invited into her bedroom. Why was she fighting it?

He pushed open the door and stepped in ahead of her, whistling through his teeth. "Nice." His eyes were on the blond sleigh bed, complete with a beige velvet comforter that invited stroking. "I may never leave, darlin'."

"Tonight only. We agreed."

Nick turned to her, wearing a wolfish grin. "Actually, we agreed for however long it lasts."

Had she agreed to that just by inviting him in? Miri lifted a shoulder, dismissing the disagreement. He might or might not agree, but they were on a night-by-night basis, with no guarantees.

"Let me help you with that. I'll bet that virgin wool is scratchy when wet."

Miri stepped away from him, hoping her cool expression hid the heat spiraling through her as her mind conjured up an entirely different use for virgin wool on wet places. "I can handle it."

"I know, but it's more fun if I do it." Nick cocked his head, winking. "C'mon."

She stood still, holding her arms loosely at her sides. The first feather-soft touch of his fingers at the waistband of her skirt made her stomach quiver. She sucked in a breath as he pulled the sweater slowly from the skirt, an inch at a time, until her waist was bared. He moved the sweater higher, revealing her stomach, which quaked continuously as his fingers stroked the exposed area.

"Your skin is so soft. Like silk. I can't wait to taste it." Nick spoke with an arrogant certainty that he would taste whatever he liked. She didn't contradict him, not wanting to. Now that she had given in to this insanity, she intended to enjoy it fully. What good were morning-after regrets without a helluva night before?

He pulled the sweater over her head, and Miri trembled at the hunger in his gaze. It made her feel vulnerable and desirable all at once. Had any man ever inspired such feelings before? Maybe her previous interludes had been so tepid because she knew all about the men selected to be lovers. There was mystery with Nick, heightening her anticipation. She didn't know what he would do next.

His lips twitched. "A beige bra too, Miri?"

She shrugged. "I like beige."

His fingers unfastened the back clasp with confidence, letting the cups lower to just above her nipples. "You need some color in your life, darlin'."

She shook her head but offered no further protest, too entranced by the way his fingers danced across the silk cups, easing them away from her small breasts with a finesse never equaled by any preceding him. Miri hardly noticed the bra as it dropped to the floor but didn't miss his fingers caressing her nipples. They hardened again, straining to meet his fingers, begging for attention. A mingled gasp-groan escaped her when he lightly pinched one. "Nick?"

He met her eyes. "Yes?"

"Kiss me."

She had barely uttered the second word when his arms were around her and her body melted against his. Miri tilted her neck to meet his descending head, and their lips touched. She was almost surprised sparks didn't flare when their flesh met. His lips were firm and demanding but also giving. She molded hers to his, sighing at the electricity humming between them. How could a kiss be so earth-shattering?

It only got better when he parted her lips with his and slid inside, playfully pushing his tongue against hers before slipping over the surface. Miri caught his tongue with hers, pinning it briefly before he broke away.

The kiss changed, getting deeper and more passionate. Nick's hands ventured from her back to her buttocks, cupping and squeezing them as he fitted her pelvis against his. His cock pressed insistently against her pussy, making her dizzy with need.

Nick's mouth moved from hers and took a leisurely trip across her cheek to her ear. Miri gasped when he twirled his tongue around the tiny hoop in her lobe, darting through the jewelry to lick a sensitive spot. She put her arms around his waist, pressing him closer. He breathed a short laugh into her ear before sucking the lobe and earring into his mouth to bite gently.

When he lifted his head, Miri surged forward, determined to see if his neck was as tempting as she had imagined. Nick jerked at the first stroke of her tongue down the column of his throat then groaned when she sucked skin between her teeth to nibble.

"Why do you scrape back your hair? I bet it's gorgeous."

She would have answered that it was practical for work, but her mouth was too busy devouring his skin. He tasted sweet, with a hint of salt, and the woodsy fragrance of his cologne contributed to his allure. She didn't hesitate in her appointed task as he unwound her hair from the bun, letting the dark brown locks fall to the middle of her back.

"God, Miri, I could lose myself in here." Nick brought a handful to his face, rubbing the strands against his cheeks. "I can't wait to see you on the bed, with your hair spread out on the pillow."

"Umm." Miri kept kissing his neck while her fingers undid the buttons of his shirt to the waistband of his pants. After parting the lapels, she let her mouth venture lower, licking a path across his chest, keeping a hand there to touch the lightly furred skin, running her fingers through his chest hair as her tongue swept over his nipple, eliciting a moan. His hand tightened on her hair, dragging her closer, and Miri surrendered to instinct.

She swirled her tongue around his nipple in small circles, gradually increasing the radius while still stroking his chest with her hand. Her other hand hooked into his waistband and one finger was bold enough to slip inside to caress his waist.

She cried out with surprise when Nick swung her into his arms to carry her to the bed. He didn't bother to push back the velvet comforter to reveal the nine-hundred-count cotton sheets underneath. The velvet cradled her back as Nick's body hovered over her front. Her breasts fit perfectly against his chest as he aligned his body over hers. She wriggled, teasing her nipples with the hair on his torso. "You're wearing too many clothes."

He cupped the back of her head, bending her neck to take control of her mouth. "You too," he said, before touching his lips to hers. The kiss was slow, with each stroke of his tongue branding her as his. She was aware of the possessiveness in his actions and reveled in it but refused to focus on the implications of giving him more power in the liaison than she should.

He eased away from her long enough to strip off his shirt, remove his belt and unfasten his pants, leaving the zipper and button of his trousers open. Miri lifted her hips as he fumbled for the zipper at the back of the skirt, easing the passage of the garment.

Nick touched her thighs, stroking the bare flesh. "I didn't figure you for a garter belt girl."

She squirmed as he ran a thumb over the beige garter belt before rubbing the silky hose on her thigh. Should she ruin the illusion and tell him she had resorted to an old-fashioned garter belt and thigh-highs because her last pair of pantyhose had ripped? No. "I need a surprise or two. Keeps things interesting."

"That it does." His hand moved higher, past the garter belt and bare skin, to her panties. They were beige too, but he made no comment.

Miri arched her hips when he ran his thumb down her slit, exciting every nerve centered there. Moisture accompanied the motion, and the panties seemed to chafe unbearably against her pussy.

Nick grew bolder, penetrating the elastic side of the panty to caress her pussy. "You're so wet."

"I want you." She was going to go insane if he didn't move along soon. She groaned as his thumb slipped inside her, probing her entrance. "Please."

"Not yet."

She gnashed her teeth when he pulled away again, this time to remove her panties. She reached for the clip on one of the garters, but his hand stayed hers. "I'll take care of it." Nick dispensed with the garter belt and panties quickly, leaving only the thigh-highs.

Miri lay there watching him, wondering what he planned next. Should she take the initiative? She wasn't shy, but there was something so manly about Nick that it precluded her feeling confident enough to demand what she wanted. He might have a dominant personality, but more important, he made her want to submit to his whims.

She reached out, running her hand up and down his bicep. "What do you want me to do?"

"Nothing. I just want to look at you." Nick nudged her thighs wider so he could kneel between them. His gaze never wavered from her pussy as he parted it with one hand. The cool air on heated flesh induced a shiver in Miri, and she held her breath, wondering if she would feel his tongue on her.

Instead, a finger from his other hand circled her clit slowly as he bent forward. His tongue rasped wetly across one of her swollen nipples, teasing her unbearably. He sucked the bud deeper into his mouth as his fingers mimicked the movement to plunge deep into her pussy. Miri arched her hips, straining for more of his hand.

Nick complied with her unspoken request by thrusting his fingers in and out of her while circling her clit with firm strokes. His tongue laved her nipple, and she squirmed under the passionate onslaught. She was so hungry for him, just aching everywhere. It no longer seemed foolish to rush into a fling. Now she couldn't get there fast enough. "Please, Nick. I need you."

He lifted his head from her breast but took his time withdrawing from her pussy, stroking her for another minute before relenting. She was slick with need when he stood up to remove his pants. The sight of his thick cock flooded her pussy with moisture. Miri imagined stroking him, tracing her fingers down the throbbing veins of his shaft and caressing the mushroom head as it spasmed against her hand. She watched impatiently as he pulled a condom from his pocket to sheath his cock before returning to her.

Nick took up the same position between her thighs, stretching out atop her. He didn't allow his full weight to rest on her as his hand parted her pussy to guide his cock inside her. Miri cupped his buttocks, pulling his cock in as deeply as she could. Her body accepted the length of him with surprising ease considering how long it had been since she had taken a lover.

She arched her hips, meeting his first thrust. The pace was slow, inciting a surge of desire that built in ever-increasing pulses. Miri's nails formed half-moons in the flesh of his buttocks as he thrust in and out of her and was eagerly met by her each time. Nick's hand slipped between their bodies, his thumb seeking out and stroking her clit in time with his thrusts.

His cock was deep inside her, seeking to learn every inch of her pussy while his fingers memorized her clit. Miri cried out when Nick buried his mouth against her neck to bite her with more vigor than tenderness. His roughness excited her, much to her surprise. She was used to polite lovemaking, not the uninhibited variety that Nick seemed so adroit at.

She closed her eyes, struggling to contain a cry of pleasure as her pussy contracted around him. Convulsions swept through her, emanating from deep in her womb and squeezing his cock to milk every last drop of satisfaction from him. The world looked fuzzy when viewed through the haze of passion obscuring her vision, and her breathing was heavy. It was difficult to draw in a deep breath as she hovered on the edge of coming, just before plunging forward. A cry escaped her as her body went rigid with release.

Spasms shook her, making her pussy contract even tighter around his cock, which spasmed in time with the tremors racking her body. Miri tried to drag him inside her by digging her nails even deeper into the skin of his buttocks as afterglow started the process of making her muscles relax.

He stiffened against her, thrusting frantically a couple of times before staying deep inside her. Nick seemed to make no effort to conceal his husky groan of fulfillment as he let loose his satisfaction. His cock released in spurts that filled her with contentment, renewing milder spasms inside her core. Their bodies shook in time with each other for what might have been seconds or hours, uniting them as one for that short time.

When it was over, he didn't withdraw from her. Nick turned on his side, bringing Miri with him, and tucking her body close to his. He brushed a kiss across her forehead, murmured, "Thank you," and held her.

How did she respond? She wanted to weep with the pleasure he had given her. Never had it been so good. What was it about Nick that completely fulfilled her, when no other man had?

As he slipped into sleep, emitting soft snores, Miri cautioned herself to be careful. Nick was dangerous to her ordered life and sheltered heart. If he could breach her body so easily, what could he do to her carefully controlled emotions?

THREE

IRI AWOKE ALONE, FINDING a note and the slight indent his head had left on the pillow the only proof he had been there. That, and the minor aches of gratification. The twinges were more pronounced when she leaned forward to retrieve the note.

Sorry I can't be here when you wake up, but I had an appointment I couldn't cancel. Be ready at seven. We're doing things my way tonight.

Nick

She frowned at the note, questioning the veracity of his vague appointment. Had it been an excuse to leave, to avoid the awkward conversation that might have awaited him if he had been there when she awoke? His high-handed tone didn't please her either. How dare he issue a dictate? She should make plans with someone else tonight, to be gone when he came around. That would show him she wasn't at his disposal.

Miri knew she wouldn't stand him up as she climbed from the bed, ill-at-ease from her nakedness. The T-shirt she normally wore to bed lay over the beige armchair in the corner. For however long this fling lasted, the old T-shirt could stay there. He was too intoxicating to cut short this . . . whatever it was . . . prematurely.

Refreshed by the previous night, she strolled to the French doors and opened them, squinting as sunshine flooded the room. Still naked, she took a step onto her balcony to survey the neighborhood. It wasn't quite eight, but several neighbors were engaged in weekend chores as children played on the streets.

She leaned against the wooden rail, hugging her arms over her breasts, wondering what prompted her to stand outside in the nude. The others in her conservative, upwardly mobile neighborhood would be shocked if they looked up at her balcony and saw her like this. They'd be even more shocked, might even shun her, if they knew the local high school science teacher had spent all night in bed with a man she hardly knew.

A giggle escaped Miri, and she clapped her hand over her mouth, alarmed by the blithe sound. It brought a return to sanity, and she hurried inside, closing the French doors behind her. For a moment, she had been a free spirit, not unlike her mother, Marnie. What was she thinking?

Last night's decision to end things with Nick at a one-night stand had been a good one. If she was going to be crazy enough to see him again, even for one more night, she had to keep a rein on her impulses, for fear that she become too much like her mother. Shaking her head with disgust at the very idea, Miri padded into the bathroom, intent on showering and slipping into clothes as soon as possible. Naïvely perhaps, she believed she could conceal the secret thoughts plaguing her mind simply by hiding her body under garments.

AGAINST HER BETTER JUDGMENT, she was waiting for Nick by six forty-five, pacing the house, pausing every few minutes to stare at the grandfather clock in the entryway, mutter under her breath and mentally chastise her foolishness once more.

Her internal cautions to be sensible did nothing to slow her racing heart when her doorbell rang at seven. With features schooled in a composed arrangement, Miri opened the door to Nick and forgot how to breathe. The black T-shirt hugged his arms and torso indecently, revealing every flex and bulge as he moved. The faded jeans, now a worn gray, clung to his legs like a second skin. Her hands itched to test the fabric to see if it was as soft as it appeared. She knew from experience that underneath she would find rock-hard flesh.

"You look delicious," he said, stepping over the threshold without waiting for her to issue an invitation. Nick leaned forward to kiss her, lightly stroking her lips with his tongue. Straightening, he towered over her again, so close she could feel his body heat.

She longed to melt against him but held herself erect by sheer willpower. "Thank you." Did he really consider this pale yellow sheath delicious? Bought to wear to an Easter service she had planned to attend with an ex-lover, the dress had gone unused when they had split days before the holiday.

He nodded. "Too dressy though. Do you have jeans?" Before she could respond, he said, "Go change."

Miri glared at him. Now was the time to nip his bossiness in the bud. "Don't be so patronizing. I've been making my own decisions for a long time, so I don't need your input on my wardrobe."

Nick's eyes widened. "Sorry, darlin'. I meant nothing by it. I want you to be comfortable. Where we're going, jeans are the norm, but it's up to you."

Put like that, her anger faded. "I'll be right back." Miri returned to her room, half-expecting Nick to follow for a repeat performance of last night. To her disappointment, as she slipped on her sole pair of blue jeans, still stiff with newness, he never made an appearance. She deliberately loitered over selecting a top, hoping he would come in, but he didn't.

With a sigh of disgust at her actions, she chose a beige square-necked tunic made of a gauzy fabric, suggesting more than it truly showed, while simultaneously slipping her feet into loafers. When she found Nick in the living room, he whistled. She extended her arms, doing a complete circle. "Does this meet your approval?"

"You bet, darlin'." He stood up and put an arm around her waist on the way to the door. His hand slipped inside her back pocket, and he winced. "Those jeans sure are stiff, unless your ass is that firm."

His words should have appalled her but instead she had to stifle a laugh. "They're new. I've only worn them once, on a field trip with the seniors last year."

He made no further comment as they left her house until Miri headed in the direction of her Saab. He tightened his grip on her pocket, steering her left to a gleaming red motorcycle parked at the curb. "We'll take my Concours."

Miri was already shaking her head even as he continued to bring her with him across her front lawn. "I've never ridden one before."

"It's about time, don't you think?"

"No, I—"

He ignored her objections by thrusting a helmet into her hands. "Try this on for size, Miri."

"Nick, I'm not riding on this—" She gasped when he pushed the helmet on her head, squashing her bun.

He pushed up the face shield and leaned forward to steal a kiss. "Live a little." His eyes twinkled. "Unless you're scared?"

Hell, yes, she was scared, but not about to admit it. Miri firmed her trembling lips, nodded just once and cinched the strap of the helmet under her chin. "Let's go."

Nick's laugh was rich with joy and too contagious. She had to bite her tongue to keep from chuckling along with him. At least the moment of mirth tempered her nerves, and she was almost relaxed by the time Nick put on his helmet and directed her to sit on the seat behind him after he climbed on.

Her hands shook when she grasped his shoulders to steady herself while mounting the seat. The position was odd, and she clutched him tighter when he started the motorcycle. The Kawasaki seemed to roar like an injured beast, and she was two seconds from backing down from his challenge when he shifted into gear and took them onto the road.

Miri's eyes widened with shock when the vibrations of the seat transmitted to her pussy. Without thought, she shifted positions to feel more of the power, loosening her death grip on Nick's neck in the process.

She spared a glance for the road, deciding she didn't like the way the lines whipped by with nauseating quickness but otherwise enjoying the ride. It was difficult to remain in fear for her life when the engine's vibrations kept her constantly aroused, just shy of an orgasm.

Nick detoured from Main Street to an area of town she never frequented. If any place in Poplin Hills could be considered seedy, it was the strip of establishments on Route 7. Her apprehension grew when he slowed down the bike to turn into Hooch's, a local tavern with colorful clientele. She'd never been inside, but rumors abounded of drunken brawls, marriage-ending events and other horrors taking place there every night of the week. No decent citizen would step foot inside.

All those thoughts ran through her mind when Nick parked

by the door beside a beaten-up black motorcycle, but she didn't utter a word when he helped her from the bike and removed her helmet. She had taciturnly agreed to let Nick set the rules for tonight. It was too late to argue now. She just hoped they survived the night without anyone connected to the school seeing her at Hooch's.

AS MIRI TOOK A seat at a table shrouded by shadows in the corner of the room, she swore she could still feel the vibration of the engine through her body. Her damp pussy throbbed in time with her heart, seeking release. Would anyone notice if she pushed Nick down across the table and had her way with him right there? Surveying the dim interior, clouded with smoke, thick with partiers, she couldn't say with absolute certainty they would. It was the sort of place where one could do just about anything without having the other patrons look askance.

"What would you like?"

"Chard . . . beer, please." When in Rome . . .

Miri's gaze remained on Nick's tight form as he moseyed up to the mahogany bar to place their orders. Her eyes narrowed when a blonde sitting on a stool gave him an enthusiastic greeting that included a wet kiss on the lips. Was she jealous of the bimbo? How could she be, considering she had no emotional ties to Nick?

Nonetheless, the sting of jealousy bit into her when the blonde climbed off the stool to plaster herself against Nick. Miri bunched her hands into fists atop her thighs, fighting the urge to march over and rip every bleached hair out of the slut's head.

Her strong reaction jarred Miri back to reality. She wasn't the kind of woman to get into a barroom brawl, especially over a man she had spent just one night with. Her anger switched to simmer as Nick brushed off the woman, got their drinks and returned to the table. She struggled to hide any hint of how she felt behind an aloof smile when he sat down.

"You didn't say tap or bottle, so I took a guess." He pushed a mug of draft beer across the scarred black table.

She lifted it, took an enthusiastic gulp and managed to hide a grimace of distaste. "Who was the woman at the bar?" Her frosty tone pleased her.

A hint of red might have tinged his cheeks. It was difficult to tell with the low lighting. "Um, a friend."

"You should have invited your *friend* to join us. I hate for her to be alone."

Nick shifted, looking uncomfortable. "I'm sure Chloe won't be lonely long."

"Hmm." She took another sip of the beer, finding it easier to tolerate with each drink. "What do you do here, besides drink?"

"Dance, play pool." He shrugged. "Hang out."

She wasn't accustomed to hanging out. Miri liked plans for everything. She always knew which movie she was going to watch at the theater before going, always reserved activities well in advance when going on vacation and never changed her mind about anything at the last minute. Drumming her fingers on the table, she scanned the bar again, noticing one of the pool tables was free. "Teach me how to play pool." What she really wanted to do was request he take her home and fuck her until she forgot her own name, but held back. They were having a civilized fling, which included the pretense of dating.

"Sure. Go hold the table, and I'll get the balls from Belle."

Miri took her mug with her to the table and stood by it with a hand on the edge, not sure if she was holding it properly. This time, Nick picked a spot several stools down from Chloe as he conversed with the mid-forties woman behind the bar. Soon, he returned with pool balls.

As he racked them, he asked, "You've never played?"

"No." The closest she had come had been the times Marnie left her in the car while she went in to drink at various bars. Miri shuddered slightly, remembering the numerous nights she had fallen asleep in various old cars, waiting for her mother to stumble out at closing time. "It never appealed to me. Until now."

"Fair enough. I'll let you break."

"Break?"

"Grab a cue and go to the other end of the table."

When Miri had selected a green cue from the wall and stood on the opposite end from Nick, he rolled a white ball to her. She had seen enough on television to know to chalk the cue. After finishing, she figured out where to put the ball and assumed breaking was the act of scattering the balls after he took away the rack holding them.

The cue was clumsy in her hands as she maneuvered it into position to hit the ball. Before she could make her shot, he moved behind her, standing so close she could feel his cock pressing into her buttocks. "Now what?" The breathless question sounded coy, not logical, as she had intended.

"Don't clench the cue so tightly." He put his hand over hers, loosening her grip while repositioning her hold. His other hand rested briefly on her hip before taking possession of her free hand, which he placed on the table, positioning it exactly. "Rest the cue here, but lightly. You want to be unrestrained when you shoot." He kept his hands over hers, demonstrating the way she should shoot. "Keep your motions fluid."

To her disappointment, Nick withdrew to let her make the

shot. As soon as he stopped touching her, she forgot everything he had shown her. The cue barely touched the ball, sending it only a couple of inches off its straight course, without getting anywhere near the triangle of balls at the other end of the table. She groaned, ready to quit.

"My turn." Nick took a cue and held it with confidence born of practice. Miri's eyes didn't stray as he leaned over the table to make his shot. The way his buttocks clenched in the tight jeans dried out her mouth. The beer she gulped did little to provide relief but kept her from uttering a moan when he completed his shot, making his body one streamlined work of art. The kind meant to be touched, not hung on a wall and admired from a distance.

The cue ball scattered the others when it slammed into their midst, causing three to drop into pockets immediately. He looked over his shoulder. "It's still my turn, but why don't you go ahead?"

She shook her head, in no hurry to end his turn. He was delicious enough to watch all night. "Play by the rules."

He started to walk past her but turned to pull her against him and press his mouth to hers. Miri's first thought was of protesting the public kiss. Her second was all about the kiss itself. She wrapped her free arm around his waist, trying to pull him closer. His mouth devoured hers as his tongue feathered against her lips.

When he pulled away, his grin was full of smug arrogance and a healthy dose of satisfaction. "Darlin', I've always found it more fun to break the rules." He moved past, leaving her with a lingering squeeze on her bottom.

The balls seemed to disappear with lightning speed as Nick set about putting them into the pockets. She watched raptly each time his muscles bunched or flexed, studied his expression for clues of his mood and felt the moisture in her pussy spread. By the time he knocked the eight ball into the corner pocket, a light sheen of perspiration misted her body and she was light-headed with arousal.

"Another?" he asked, rounding up the balls from under the table, where they had dropped after going into the pockets.

She shook her head. "Where's the ladies' room?"

"Down the hall." He pointed to a sign across the room. "Are you sure? You didn't get to play much."

"It's fine." She abandoned her beer and rushed to the restroom, shaking with the effort not to make a fool of herself. Her body ached for his. She was hotter than she had ever been, dripping with need. A few minutes of privacy was all she needed to collect herself. She hoped.

The restroom was as dim as the rest of the bar but not as smoky. There were two stalls, and she chose the handicapped one because it was closer. Miri locked the door and leaned against it, taking deep breaths that did nothing to calm her. This night had been nothing but foreplay, and she was ready for the main event. The only thing that had stopped her from begging Nick to leave was she didn't think she could wait to get back to her place.

The main door opened, and she tried to halt her rapid breathing. Her inhalation turned to a gasp when Nick peeked over her stall. "What are you doing? This is the ladies' room."

He grinned, unrepentant. "Open up."

She shook her head, even as her fingers obeyed his command and turned the lock. A flutter of common sense had her reaching for the door as he swung it open. "You can't . . . we can't."

"Remember the rules, darlin'." Nick entered the stall with her, locking the door. He was too close for rational thought as he pinned her against the side of the stall, pressing his mouth to hers. "Break them," he said, right before kissing her.

Propriety dictated she push him away, but her body had other ideas. Miri clung to Nick, running her fingers through his hair with one hand while resting the other at his waist. A moan escaped her when Nick's hand slid under the hem of her tunic to caress her stomach. His tongue thrust inside her mouth, and she met it eagerly, parrying his attempts to explore all of her.

One of his hands moved higher, cupping her breast through her bra, while his thumb rubbed over her swollen nipple, inflaming it with the lacy fabric. She nipped his tongue, earning a pinch that served only to heighten her arousal. Her hips arched of their own accord, bringing her dripping pussy against his cock, separated only by the fabric of their jeans. The barrier was too much, and she wanted to strip off their clothes and have him pin her to the wall.

Nick broke the kiss to sweep his mouth down her throat, pausing to bite the bend of her neck with just enough pressure to elicit a moan. Miri tightened her fingers in his hair, trying to halt his descent as he slid lower. He ignored her temporary resistance, and she stopped fighting when he pushed her tunic above her breasts. His tongue swept into the valley of her cleavage, modest as it was, and he inhaled. "You smell like flowers," he said against her skin, sparking flicks of heat with every breathy word.

"You smell like sex." The blunt words shocked her, but he didn't seem taken aback by her uttering them. And it was true. Nick smelled, tasted, walked and talked S-E-X. She couldn't help responding. Urgent hands tugged his T-shirt up so she could caress his abdomen, which fluttered under her hand. His cock pressed more insistently against her pussy through the jeans, and she parted her thighs wider to allow it to nestle deeper.

To her surprise, he shifted her suddenly, pressing her against the wall and supporting her on one of his thighs while she braced her hands on his shoulders. His movements were smooth and quick when he released the back clasp of her bra and pushed the cups above her breasts, along with the tunic. Once freed, her breasts strained for his touch, and Miri's nipples tingled with warmth.

Nick's mouth was gentle but with a hint of roughness when he took possession of one nipple. The bead disappeared into his mouth, where he flicked his tongue over the tip, causing her to stifle a cry of passion. Miri dug her nails into his shoulders, pulling him closer still while writhing against his thigh, seeking relief for the inferno blazing inside her pussy. "Nick, I can't take this." They had to leave, find the nearest bed and satiate each other.

He lifted his head to stare into her eyes. "Yeah, you can, darlin'. Trust me." Then his hands moved to her waistband, dispensing with the button and zipper to plunge his hand inside. His fingers stroked her pussy through the silky panties she wore, and Miri tossed her head from side to side, desperate for relief, as his fingers teased her clit through the silk. "Please, Nick. Let's get out of here."

"Easy." His hand left her pants, and he lowered her back to her feet. Miri experienced a dart of disappointment, despite it having been her request to stop and find somewhere else more private. Her discontent changed to confusion when Nick got on his knees before her.

Her eyes widened when he pulled down her jeans and panties. Somehow, she managed to remain coherent enough to kick off her loafers and step out of them.

There was no mistaking his intentions as he leaned forward, tongue extended. She twined a hand in his hair, not sure if she wanted to push him away or pull him closer. He didn't allow her to choose, lunging forward suddenly, tongue seeking out her heat. Miri closed her eyes with a gasp, leaning against the stall wall for support as Nick's tongue sought out all her secret places, paying special attention to her clit, swollen with need.

The moist swipes of his tongue probing her opening made Miri ball her hands into fists to keep from shouting. Nick pressed his tongue deeper inside her pussy. She shifted with restless energy, needing more than his intimate kiss. She wanted him inside her.

Nick seemed to have read her thoughts, because he brought a hand between her thighs. His tongue abandoned her opening, leaving her temporarily bereft, until two of his fingers plunged inside to take its place. It wasn't his cock, but the digits were almost enough to satisfy her. When Nick swirled his tongue around her clit, she cried out while mindlessly thrusting against his face as spasms in her pussy built in intensity.

She was on the brink of release when the outer door opened. Miri's eyes snapped open, and she froze as footsteps went past their stall, though Nick continued to lick her pussy. She pulled on his hair, trying to get his attention, but he remained focused on his task. "Nick," she said so quietly she barely heard it herself as the door to the stall beside them closed and the woman engaged the lock.

She couldn't help seeing Nick kneeling on the floor and must know what they were doing. Shame burned through Miri, firing her cheeks, but another sensation fought for supremacy. It was the wild impulse to ignore the other woman's presence, and it was winning. Nick's passionate ministrations, continuing without pause, helped it along toward victory. With a sigh of defeat, she closed her eyes, struggled not to breathe too heavily and let his tongue work its magic.

The woman was in the process of washing her hands when the orgasm swept over Miri. Try as she did, she couldn't keep in a moan of satisfaction. Every muscle in her body quivered with release, and she slumped against Nick, who was still caressing her with slow strokes, coaxing every drop of pleasure from her.

The outer door closed, bringing Miri back to a semblance of awareness as Nick got to his feet. Her actions should shock her, and they did, but she was too limp with gratification to make an issue of what they had done.

He kissed her gently on the mouth before saying, "That was intense. There's a real wanton underneath that schoolmarm exterior, Miri."

"Only with you," she admitted, leaning against him with her arms on his shoulders. His hands moved between their bodies to free his cock from his jeans. Miri kept her head against his chest as he ripped open a foil packet taken from his pocket and covered his cock.

Her thighs parted wider when he shifted into position, aligning his cock with her pussy. With a soft gasp, Miri welcomed him fully inside. After the last orgasm, she didn't know if she could survive another, but he set about proving she could, using his cock and hands to stroke her to a fever pitch. As her pussy contracted around him, she tossed her head, biting hard on her tongue to hold in a cry.

Nick filled the silence with a groan as he came, pulling her so tightly against him that they were almost one person for a moment, especially when their heartbeats thundered in time with each other.

When it was over, he held her for a long moment before pressing a kiss to her neck. "Your place or mine?"

She was exhausted and opened her mouth to tell him she couldn't

do this again tonight, needing time to recover, but her answer caught
her by surprise. "Yours. I want to see where you live."

"It's your standard bachelor pad, but it has a bed."

"That's all we need."

AS HE'D SAID, HIS apartment was standard fare—white walls, brown
carpet and a single bedroom, which they didn't make it to. As soon
as Nick closed the door, he swept Miri into his arms and carried
her to the overstuffed leather sofa. She stretched out on the sump-
tuous cushions, supporting her head on an arm bent behind her.
She smiled up at him as he stood over her. Her eyes focused on the
bulge in his pants, and she licked her lips.

Nick settled onto the couch, straddling her, making his cock
dig into her stomach. He braced his hands on either side of her
head and leaned forward to kiss her. Miri opened her mouth when
his lips touched hers, changing the kiss from casual to intense by
sweeping her tongue inside his. She brought both hands forward
to splay across his chest, pulling him closer.

Nick groaned when she sucked his lower lip into her mouth,
and she grasped handfuls of his shirt to keep from vocalizing her
own pleasure. Her pussy ached with need, despite the pleasure
he'd already given her, and she arched her hips, finding no gratification in empty space.

Frustrated, Miri tore her mouth from Nick's before he could
pin her tongue with his. "I want you." It was liberating to be so
blunt with her emotions. So liberating, she tried it again. "I want
your cock inside me."

Nick seemed surprised by her words but nodded. "Sure, darlin'.
Whenever you're ready." He winked.

Miri couldn't hide a grin of satisfaction at his startled look when she shoved against his shoulders. He went tumbling off the couch, and she followed, now straddling him as they lay on the floor. She tugged at his T-shirt. "Now would be appreciated."

He groaned. "Can I have a minute to catch my breath? That was a helluva ride."

"No, but it will be." She ignored his requests to take it easy as she pulled at his shirt until it was over his head. When he was bared from the waist up, she let her hands roam over his chest, raking her nails across his nipples. She enjoyed his sharp inhalation so much she scratched the tender nubs again.

"Damn." He didn't sound angry. Rather, surprise and something more colored his tone. Enjoyment, perhaps?

Miri bent her head so she could focus her attention on the button and zipper of his jeans. They yielded to her determined hands with a rasp, and she opened the pants to reveal her prize. Nick's underwear posed a slight deterrent, and she had to tug at the waistband of his jeans and briefs a few times until he cooperated by lifting his hips.

In her impatience, she got the pants no lower than his knees. Seated across his shins, she shifted slightly to maximize her mobility. Then Miri looked up at him, finding Nick watching her with amused indulgence. She wanted to wipe that expression off his face, wanted him to feel the same need she felt, just as urgently. She hated being vulnerable, but if she was going to be, she refused to experience it alone.

"I'm going to fuck you now," she said, almost conversationally.

He folded his hands behind his head. "Is that right?"

She nodded just once.

His grin held more than a small measure of self-satisfaction. "Wouldn't you be more comfortable on the bed?"

"I'll be plenty comfortable on your cock," she retorted.

A hearty laugh escaped him. "By all means, go for it. I'm not going to stop you."

"No, you aren't." He still wasn't feeling the same urgency, but that was about to change. Miri leaned forward, catching a brief glimpse of his stunned expression just before his face disappeared from her line of sight. He jumped when her lips touched the head of his cock, but she spared no mercy for him to adjust to the erotic intrusion. In a smooth motion, Miri engulfed his cock in her mouth, somehow accommodating all of him.

He tasted like come and latex, along with something uniquely him. It wasn't completely unpleasant, and she soon forgot her initial reaction to his flavor when his cock convulsed in her mouth. She began to suck, working her head up and down, and knew she had provoked the response she wanted when he started pumping his hips.

Miri had her hands braced on his thighs, but she brought up one to hold the base of his cock, squeezing lightly. Nick groaned when she moved her mouth in a circle around his shaft, applying more suction to the head.

His thrusts increased in speed, and he sounded hoarse when he spoke. "I'm about to come, darlin'. You're too good."

She bit him on the head, scraping her teeth across the sensitive flesh. When he uttered a wordless protest, she lifted her head to smile at him. "You aren't coming yet."

He growled, glaring at her. "Are you playing with me?"

Miri didn't respond verbally. Instead, she let her gaze settle on his cock while her hands dispensed with the tunic. Nick reached up to help with her bra, and she smacked his hand lightly. "This is my show, Nick."

He laughed, though it contained more strain than amusement. "I guess I'll just watch."

"For now." She unfastened the bra and tossed it onto the floor beside the tunic. Her sense of order winced at the mess, but desire overrode her natural prissiness, and she turned her attention to the jeans. Her hands shook with anticipation, making it slow work to strip her jeans and underwear down below her knees. Though they restrained her legs, she had no time to waste getting them off.

"Condoms?"

Nick pointed downward. "Right pocket of my jeans."

Miri reached behind her awkwardly, feeling for a bulge in the denim. When she found the pocket, she plunged her fingers inside and pulled out three condoms. With haste, she tore one off the strip. It resisted opening so she used her teeth. Her urgent need was disquieting, but she was too immersed in it to back off, cool down and think about all the reasons why she shouldn't be attacking Nick—least of all, she wasn't like this. Clearly, she was when with Nick.

His cock jerked at her feathery touch when she rolled the condom down the shaft. Miri paused to caress his head, applying a small amount of pressure to the sensitive V until he lunged upward, his teeth clenched. Satisfied he finally felt the same driving desire as she did, she scooted higher up his body.

If not for the jeans hindering her legs, she could have been on him in seconds. It took close to a minute to position her pussy atop his cock and get a sense of balance. When she was centered, Miri sank down on him, and they both moaned when his cock filled her.

She dug her nails into his chest where she'd braced them and began arching up and down. "That feels so good." Miri circled her hips while clenching her pussy around his cock.

"You've got that right, darlin'. I could stay in your hot little pussy for hours."

A bead of sweat dripped into her eyes, but she didn't bother to wipe it away. "I can't wait that long."

"Me neither," he admitted with a grunt while driving forcefully inside her. His cock spasmed, making her womb quake in response. Miri was on the edge of coming, and when she scooted forward a smidge and arched her back, his cock rubbed right against her clit as she rode him. Their frantic thrusts pushed them closer to the edge, and she suddenly found herself falling over it.

The heat of his liquid satisfaction spread to her through the condom as he climaxed, and it triggered more convulsions in her pussy. She tightened her muscles around his cock and crested the peak of her orgasm, gradually slowing the speed of her thrusts until the last bit of tension faded, and she collapsed on top of him, breathless.

They didn't speak, and she was grateful not to have to make conversation. At that moment, she was still out of control, a sensation that terrified her. She needed time to gather her composure, which was impossible with his cock slowly waning inside her. After the way she had just behaved, she couldn't face him and act normally. It was better to hide her face against his chest and try to forget how wild she had been. That was easier to plan than execute with her body still glowing from the amazing release, and her inhibitions temporarily freed from restraint.

She knew, lying atop him, that she couldn't let this happen again. If he could make her lose control this way, she could easily end up like her mother. Miri couldn't allow herself to lose her hard-won self-respect on the altar of desire.

But when his cock hardened a few minutes later, and his hands cupped her breasts to rub her nipples, it never occurred to her to refuse him. In a matter of moments, she was swept away again, forgetting her previous resolutions.

FOUR

*N*ICK WAVED OFF THE last of the guys trying to talk him into going to the bar while dialing Miri's number. He hadn't seen her in the three days he had been on duty, hadn't even called her, but hadn't been able to think about anything except her during that time. The last two weeks of their affair had flown by, it seemed, and he still hadn't gotten enough of her.

It scared the hell out of him, but here he was, calling her after only three days of self-imposed silence, when he had been trying to make it a full week. Would she be happy to hear from him or irritated he had gone so long without speaking to her?

He grimaced as the phone rang, reminding himself she hadn't tried to call him at the station either, though it would have been a simple matter of looking up the number in the phone book. Perhaps she was managing to compartmentalize their casual fling better than he was.

She answered on the third ring, rasping, "Hello."

"Miri?"

"Yes. Nick?"

"You sound awful." He winced at his honesty.

"Thanks." She coughed before continuing. "I picked up a bug at school."

"I was going to bring by Chinese food, but maybe I'd better bring you soup instead." Smooth invitation. He shook his head at the way the words had emerged, leaving her little choice.

Silence filled the line for a moment. "I'm sick."

"I won't catch anything. Hearty New England stock, remember?" It was clear from her tone she was trying to get rid of him, so why wasn't he accepting that gracefully?

Again, she hesitated, finally saying, "I'm not feeling up to anything . . . if you know what I mean?"

His voice lowered, becoming more reassuring. "That's fine, darlin'. I'll bring food, DVDs and pampering."

Her reluctance was evident, along with her weariness, when she spoke again. "Fine."

Nick didn't like the surge of relief that swept through him, nor the way his stomach clenched with anticipation at seeing her. He forced himself to sound neutral when replying. "Great. Do you want Chinese food or chicken soup?"

"Egg-drop soup sounds good."

"Right. I'll see you soon, darlin'." Nick hung up before she could retract her acquiescence, sensing she was on the verge of telling him not to come over. He didn't want to scrutinize too closely why he was so desperate to see her or why his experiment of imposing some distance between them had failed. Nor did he want to think about why he couldn't get her out of his mind or how it had hurt to know she thought he only wanted to come by for sex. It was a logical assumption on her part, since every date they'd been on had ended with them tangled in the sheets of one of their beds, so there was no reason for him to feel wounded.

No reason he wanted to examine anyway.

MIRI MADE LITTLE EFFORT with her appearance before Nick's arrival, deciding to let him see her complete with red nose, swollen eyes and an old robe she'd had since college. This sudden move from casual sex into relationship realm alarmed her, maybe because she wanted to move to the next level as she never had before. When a man got too close, she'd had no trouble sending him on his way but didn't feel the same compulsion to do so with Nick.

Her insides had warmed in a disconcerting way when he'd said he was going to come by just to pamper her. No one had ever brought her soup or taken care of her when she was sick. It was disconcerting to have her casual lover showing such tender concern.

When the doorbell rang, the thoughts were still swirling through her mind as she tried to decide what was the best way to get rid of Nick and her own treacherous longings.

All thoughts of sending him on his way flew out of her brain when she opened the door to see Nick holding a large teddy bear under one arm and a bag of Chinese food in his hand. The bear held a heart that said "Get Well." Before she could school her reaction, she was reaching for the bear and cuddling it against her.

"You like it?" His boyish need to please was evident in his expression and the way he shifted from foot to foot.

Miri nodded, incapable of speech for a moment. Nick slipped past her to set the Chinese food and a bag of DVDs on the coffee table before turning back to take her in his arms.

Sick as she was, her body responded to his proximity, and it was strange to have him press a chaste kiss to her forehead instead of receiving the passionate greeting she had expected. Somehow, she ended up cuddled against him, with the bear forming an awkward barrier between them. Tears burned behind her eyes, and Miri blinked rapidly to dissolve them, not certain why she wanted to cry.

"C'mon. You should be resting." He guided her to the couch, seating her on the middle cushion. Looking sheepish, he touched the bear briefly. "Silly, huh?"

She shook her head. "It's wonderful." Her voice was wet with suppressed tears, but at that moment, she was unable to hide her emotions and hoped he would chalk it up to her illness. "Thank you."

Nick shrugged, as if trying to push aside his embarrassment. He didn't respond except to remove a Styrofoam container from the plastic bag and hand it to her. "Egg-drop soup." A plastic soup spoon followed before he arranged two boxes of food and chopsticks on the table.

Miri made a production of opening the soup and examining the contents before taking a small spoonful, desperate to avoid his eyes lest he see the vulnerability in hers. She only looked up when he called her name, jiggling two rental cases.

"I wasn't sure what you liked, so I picked up a chick flick and an action movie. Which will it be?"

She pointed to the action movie, in no mood to have her already raw emotions exposed further by any heartrending issue the chick flick might explore. Nick put it in her DVD player before joining her on the couch.

As they watched the movie, eating, no words passed their lips. When Miri had eaten as much of the soup as she could, she put the lid on and leaned back against the cushion, carefully resting her head on his shoulder. Nick put aside his food to take her into his arms. A spark of electricity arced between them, but his demeanor was one of caretaker rather than lover as he held her.

She relaxed into him, enjoying his embrace more than she should. It was a foreign experience to have someone else care about her well-being, to take care of her. That it would be Nick, the man she was supposed to be having a fling with, made it even stranger. He wasn't supposed to be the sensitive type. All brawn with a massive dose of sex appeal—that was his persona. He wasn't supposed to upset her preconceived notions and make her start to fall for him.

Her eyes, drooping, snapped open at the thought. Miri tensed, almost pulling away, as if she could escape her emotions just by putting some distance between them. Three days of silence on both their parts hadn't done anything to diminish her desire for him, so why did she think withdrawing from his embrace would do anything?

"Miri? Are you okay?"

Slowly she nodded, allowing her body to relax again. "I was falling asleep."

"Go ahead. I'll make sure you get to bed."

The words themselves were sexy but delivered in a nurturing manner. Miri tried to force her thoughts from her emotions to concentrate on the movie, but it was a long time before she was successful.

BY THE END OF the movie, Miri was snoring softly against him. Nick looked down at her upturned face, noting the lines of worry around her eyes, and wondered what haunted her.

She sighed in her sleep, snuggling closer. A glance at the clock revealed it was nearly ten, which meant he should get going. In other circumstances, he would have stayed with her for a few hours, but tonight he didn't feel the urge.

As he got to his feet, lifting her into his arms effortlessly, Nick acknowledged that that wasn't true when his cock swelled against his jeans. He had the desire, but her needs outweighed his wants. Never before had he experienced this curious blend of tenderness and passion for a lover. Not one of the women he had been involved with in the past had ever evoked a need in him to take care of her.

Carrying her to her room, staring down at her, Nick faced an unpleasant truth. He was in love with Miri. It didn't give him the surge of terror he expected. Instead, as he placed her under the covers and brushed a kiss against her cheek, satisfying warmth spread through him, radiating from his heart, not his cock. For the life of him, he couldn't remember right then why he had fought so long against feeling something real for a woman.

"I love you," he said in a whisper, trying out the words, liking the way they sounded. Her eyes opened briefly. She locked gazes with him for just a second before her eyes slammed closed again and her snoring increased. It was just long enough for him to catch the glint of panic in her eyes.

FIVE

S SOON AS MIRI opened her eyes the next morning, Nick's words swirled through the layers of her subconscious to lodge in the forefront of her mind. With a smothered groan, she rolled out of bed, desperate to escape her emotions. Panic was there, as it had been last night, but there was more. Was that giddy tickle in her chest happiness or simply the remnants of her cold?

Miri hurried into the bathroom, trying to deny she felt anything other than fear at Nick's confession. Her eyes revealed something different than her brain wanted to see. They were soft pools of darkness, tinged with a warm glow. Her lips tried to curve into a smile, and she had to school her expression into her most severe look, one usually reserved for recalcitrant students.

Dammit, she was pleased with Nick's words. Somehow, he had wormed his way into her life, burrowing into her heart in a way no man had ever done before. Her walls had dropped, her defenses had let her down . . . and she didn't care?

"I love you." Her lips formed the words hesitantly, and her voice was a rusty rasp in the enclosed space of the bathroom. She waited for some reaction, like the ceiling to fall on her, but nothing happened, other than a lightening in her chest.

Padding from the bathroom, forgetting about her morning ablutions, Miri continued practicing the words under her breath. Each time she said them, they came easier, until she almost thought she could say them to Nick when they next met.

HER FLEDGLING COMFORT WITH Nick's confession and her own response lasted until the next afternoon, when her phone rang. Not given to moments of intuition, it was with strange foreboding that Miri answered the telephone, every instinct screaming to ignore the out-of-area number. "Hello?"

"Miri, darling."

Her stomach churned as soon as her mother's voice came over the line. "Hello, Marnie." She'd used her mother's given name since she was eight, when Marnie had decided she looked too young to have men know she had a daughter. "How are you?" To what did she owe the phone call? Marnie kept in touch infrequently, usually only if she wanted something, like money.

"Deliriously happy."

Ah, a new man. "Oh?"

"I'm getting married."

Miri's lips curled in a cynical grimace. "You're already married."

Marnie laughed. "Oh, darling, not for long."

"What happened with Herb?" Or was it Howard? After the number of uncles and stepfathers who had paraded through Miri's life, she couldn't keep them straight.

Her mother sighed, sounding impatient. "He's so boring. He doesn't understand me at all. Can you believe he wanted me to work with him? I can't think of anything duller than sitting in an office all day."

"So you went shopping for a new husband?"

Marnie's tone sharpened. "I didn't plan it. It just sort of happened, but I couldn't stop how I felt. Craig is the one."

"Hmm."

Not picking up on Miri's skepticism, Marnie continued. "He's never been married, has no children, owns a chain of restaurants and has the most beautiful yacht. We're going to spend six months sailing around the world for our honeymoon. It's a ninety-footer, complete with a full staff—"

Miri tuned out her mother's enthusiastic description of the yacht and other material goods. It was just another match made in material heaven. One thing she could credit her mother with was Marnie's ability to trade up. She could certainly pick her targets. The thought of using men so callously turned Miri's stomach, though she had little sympathy for the men who had married her mother. They should have realized what they were getting into. Loving Marnie was no excuse to be blind to her faults.

Nothing good ever came from love. It was a lesson Miri had learned repeatedly over the years, but a moment of weakness had nearly undermined her. Whatever fragile emotional attachment she had almost allowed to grow had to be firmly squashed. Her mother's phone call and latest marriage was a timely reminder of what Miri had known most of her life. She was better off alone than allowing herself to love anyone as passionately as she could love Nick. She would lose herself in him, and for what? An emotion that couldn't possibly last. She had to protect herself, and that meant hardening her heart.

NICK POUNDED ON MIRI'S door relentlessly, knowing she was home. He had seen her car in the garage when he peeked in the window. Her avoidance of him over the past five days was about to end. He was going to force a confrontation, damn her wishes and his own fear of rejection. Limbo was worse than knowing how she felt about him, even if her feelings weren't mutual.

Finally, she opened the door, a trace of annoyance in her expression. "Nick? What's so urgent?"

He didn't wait for an invitation, instead pushing past her. She followed him, emanating arctic silence as he turned to face her in the living room. "Why have you been avoiding me?"

Miri frowned, giving every appearance of ignorance. "I don't know what you mean. I missed three days of school and have been struggling to catch up with everything."

"You haven't had time to return even one of my calls in the last five days?" He snorted. "Yeah."

"I had other priorities."

Her cool façade, such a contrast to the inferno burning inside him, was infuriating. He took a step closer, absurdly pleased by the way she stood her ground, though he wouldn't have minded some acknowledgement she wasn't as unaffected as she pretended. "Liar."

Her eyes widened. "Excuse me?"

"You're running scared." Nick shook his head. "It won't work. You have to face me sometime."

Miri turned partially away from him. "I have no idea what you're talking about."

He touched her shoulder, and she tensed at the light contact. "I know you heard me."

She shrugged him off. "Heard what?"

He pressed her back against his chest. "I told you I loved you."

Miri shook her head. "No."

"I did." He turned her resisting body so she was facing him, though she avoided his gaze. Nick lifted her chin, forcing her to look into his eyes. "I do. I love you."

Fear flared in her eyes. "You're crazy. You don't know me."

"I know all I need to."

She pulled away. "No, you don't. You don't know anything important about me. Did you know my mother has been married seven times . . . about to be eight? There was also a parade of countless uncles in my life, always a priority over me." Tears leaked from the corners of her eyes, and she brushed them away with an impatient gesture. "Do you want to know how many of them had grabby hands? How many times she ignored me when I told her?"

His stomach clenched with anger. "Give me their names. They'll never hurt you again."

She shook her head. "None of them ever really hurt me, not nearly as much as knowing my mother needed a man—any man— more than she needed to live up to her responsibility to me."

Nick reached for her, not allowing her to shove away his hands. He pulled her stiff body into his arms. "I'm sorry you had to go through that."

"It doesn't matter now. It taught me an important lesson. I don't want to love a man, and I don't want one to love me." Her expression was a perfect sheet of ice when she looked up at him. "I don't want your love, Nick. You're wasting your time trying to convince me."

He shook his head, refusing to believe. "You don't mean that. It's natural to be frightened after the experiences in your childhood, but I wouldn't hurt you."

"I know, because you'll never have the chance." Miri withdrew from him and pointed to the door. "You need to leave now."

"Miri—"

"Go. I don't want to see you again."

Nick stared at her for half a minute, searching for a crack in her veneer but finding none. His shoulders slumped, and he took a step toward the door. "You'll change your mind. You just need time to think things through."

Miri turned away from him. "I won't. I don't want you, and I definitely don't love you."

He winced at the pain her words caused. Nick had the fleeting urge to rage at her, but it faded quickly. Nothing he could say would reach her right then, emotionally frozen as she was. He could only hope she might come to her senses and open up to him in the coming days. His happiness—and hers—depended on it. He walked away without looking back, not wanting her to see the tears misting his eyes, wondering if she was as close to weeping as he was. In her frigid state, he doubted it.

SIX

*M*IRI POURED A CUP of coffee, deliberately avoiding the gaze of Janine, the French teacher, the closest thing she had to a best friend. She hoped Janine wouldn't look up from the TV as Miri slid into a seat at the table in the staff room.

"Finally, a minute alone." Janine turned from the TV, giving Miri an assessing glance. "Spill."

Assuming a cool expression, Miri looked up from the newspaper spread across the table. "What?"

"Something's up with you. A man?"

"No."

Janine laughed. "Yeah, sure. Only a man can make you as testy and disagreeable as you've been lately."

Frowning, Miri met Janine's eyes. "I don't know what you're talking about."

"I'm talking about that delicious firefighter you were banging for a short time. Suddenly, you no longer say a thing about him, and you're a regular grouch. Clearly, a lack of sex is to blame."

"Well, aren't you full of insights today?" Miri glared at her.

Janine nodded, asking matter-of-factly, "Did he dump you?"

Miri inched up her chin. "No. As a matter of fact, he's madly in love with me." Why bother with the pretense? Janine was the only person who had even an inkling of how her childhood had been, so she would be the only one who could understand why Miri had rejected Nick.

Her green eyes sparkled with excitement. "That's fabulous. Are you keeping it hush-hush until you have a firm commitment?"

"No. I broke it off."

"What?" Janine's outburst carried throughout the room, briefly rousing the interest of Gertrude, the gym teacher, before she returned to a thick manual of physiology. "Are you out of your mind? You finally find a man worth keeping and you discard him?"

Miri drew into herself, wrapping her hands around the coffee mug to draw some warmth from it, upon finding none from her so-called friend. "You know I don't want a man, not long-term anyway."

Janine's voice lowered to a whisper when she leaned across the table, coming closer. "You aren't going to turn into your mother by daring to have a relationship, Miri. You don't really want to be alone for the rest of your life, do you? If so, it's a very bleak future you're contemplating."

She got to her feet, abandoning the coffee. "I'm happy as I am. I didn't ask for your opinion, and I'd appreciate you keeping it to yourself." Without allowing Janine the opportunity to respond, Miri swept from the staff room, refusing to look back or acknowledge the icy ball in her stomach that had formed at Janine's words. No, it wouldn't be bleak to be alone. It would be safe and predictable. No one could hurt her as long as she kept them all at arm's length. She regretted the friendship she had allowed to blossom with Janine and vowed it would end right then.

IN KEEPING WITH HER decision, she met Janine with a chill tone when the other woman stopped by her classroom a little after four. "Yes?"

"I need to tell you something—"

"I accept your apology." She stuffed papers into her eel-skin briefcase, keeping her profile turned from Janine.

"I'm not here to apologize."

Her distraught tone finally caught Miri's attention, forcing her to look up. "What's wrong?"

"There's been a fire at the country club . . . the roof collapsed." Janine's eyes were wide with apprehension, and her hands trembled when she reached out to Miri. "Two firefighters were killed, and three more have been taken to the hospital."

"Nick." Was he working a thirty-six-hour shift this week, or was it one of his three days off? She didn't know. Miri didn't question her reaction as she dropped her briefcase and scooped up her purse, fishing for car keys as she ran to the door. Janine shouted something behind her, but she didn't take time to figure out what it was as she ran through the building to the parking lot. She had to get to Nick. *Please let him be alive.*

THE HALLS AT POPLIN Hills General were crowded with friends and family members of the firefighters, making it difficult for Miri to push her way through the throng to the front desk. Three nurses engaged in various tasks ignored her for a long moment until she thumped her hand onto the counter to get their attention.

The oldest one looked up from her paperwork. "May I help you?"

"I'm here . . . is Nick . . . " She took a deep breath, struggling to compose herself so she could force out the question, almost afraid to hear the answer. "Is Nick Martin here?"

The nurse glanced at a clipboard before looking up. "He's in room 115."

Miri turned from the desk, heading down the hallway.

"Miss, you can't go back there. Only family—"

She broke into a jog, hoping to outrun the nurse's admonishment and make it to the room before anyone stopped her. The woman's voice faded as Miri moved farther away from the desk, and she dared to hope she would make it to the room.

She passed 113 and 114 before seeing a man in a blue security uniform moving toward her from the opposite end of the hall. Miri increased her pace and pushed her way into 115 as security called to her.

Her breath caught in her throat when she saw the body lying in the bed, wrapped in bandages from almost head to foot. His leg was suspended in traction, and what visible skin there was around the bandages bore blisters. She walked forward, bracing herself. The person lying there was in bad shape.

"Nick." His name was a choked whisper, and she sagged forward, wanting to touch him but afraid of hurting him. "Oh, Nick, what have I done?"

"Miri?"

She jerked with shock at his voice and spun around to find Nick standing behind her. Her mouth dropped open, and she drank in the sight of him, noticing the bandages on his arm and across his forehead. She threw herself into his arms. "You're alive."

He held her close. "I wasn't inside when the roof collapsed. I got my injuries going in with the second squad to help get out my buddies."

Sobs shook her body, and she clutched his shirt. "I thought you were dying or dead. I was such an idiot." Miri raised her head. "I could have lost you, and you never would have known—"

The door opened, admitting the guard. "You can't be in here."

Nick waved his hand. "We'll leave in just a second."

Miri turned her head in time to see the guard's stern expression fade. "Never mind. I didn't realize she was with you, Nick." He turned to the door, leaving a heavy silence in his wake.

Finally, Nick cleared his voice. "You were saying?"

She hesitated, finding her courage had deserted her at the penultimate moment. During the frantic drive to the hospital, all she could think about was how could she go on without Nick, but now that he was safe, she found it impossible to remove the last fragment of the wall protecting her heart. Instead, she asked, "Who is the man in the bed?"

"My chief, Brady Holland. I'm waiting with him until his wife arrives. She works in Portland."

"Will he make it?"

Nick sighed. "We don't know yet."

Still clutching his shirt, Miri looked up at him. "What you do is dangerous."

He nodded. "Yes. I love it, but I'd give it up if you asked me to. I finally understand how my brother could walk away from his career for his wife."

Tears trickled from her eyes, and she buried her face against his chest. "I couldn't ask that of you."

He pushed up her chin, forcing her to meet his eyes. "Haven't you figured out by now I'll do anything for you? I love you, Miri, more than I've ever loved being a firefighter. More than I've ever loved anything. I want to spend my life making you happy, if you'll let me."

The wall crumbled with what she swore was an audible crack. Miri's muscles refused to support her, and she slumped against him, letting his T-shirt absorb her tears. "I love you, Nick." The words were strange on her tongue, but she meant them with every ounce of her being. When she dared to look up, she found Nick's lips trembling and couldn't tell if his eyes were glazed with tears or if the mist was from hers. "I love you." This time, the words were easier to say. "I don't know how it happened or when, but I do love you. Can you forgive me for pushing you away?"

"It doesn't matter what happened in the past." His words carried significant meaning, not just for their history but also for her own. "All that matters is the future."

She stretched on her tiptoes to kiss him, finding herself optimistic about the future for the first time ever. With the thawing of her heart, she was free to imagine a dizzying array of possibilities in their future, and none were bleak. How could they be with Nick by her side?

BE CAREFUL WHAT YOU WISH FOR

JOANNA WYLDE

ONE

*S*ANDRA RUBBED HER HANDS together vigorously, letting the soap cut through the remnants of the massage oil. Fat old prick.

The cheap bastard probably wouldn't even pay her, not that she expected it. That's what she got for agreeing to do a private appointment with a new client. At the time it seemed like a dream come true. Edgar Williams's secretary had said her boss was desperate, had even offered to pay twice her fee.

Of course, for what he seemed to believe a massage therapist did for a living, her price was a steal. She could still feel his fat, hairy fingers gripping her ass. Why on earth would a man like that think money could possibly be enough to make her have sex with him? She'd rather be eaten by a snake!

The pipes made a moaning noise as she shut off the faucets, and she wrinkled her nose. For a couple of lawyers, Edgar and his partner didn't seem to make much. Their office was nothing more than an old converted house, and it was a dump. She grabbed at the towel to wipe her hands and shuddered as her fingers hit crust. *Yuck.* She wiped them on her jeans instead, then turned and opened the door.

"I'm out of here. You should be ashamed of yourself, Williams," she declared as she stalked out of the bathroom into the office. "I have every intention of reporting you to the Better Business Bureau—"

Her voice cut off abruptly as she took in the scene before her. Edgar stood frozen, facing a tall shadow of a man. Neither spoke.

"What's going on here?" she asked. The shadow stepped forward into the light. He was big, a man who had clearly spent a lot of time lifting weights. The clothes he wore fit poorly, as if made for a smaller man. His long, black hair was pulled back in a ponytail and his face seemed chiseled in ice. His arm moved, catching her eye.

Something glinted in his hand. *Shit*. It was a knife.

"You aren't supposed to be here," he said to her slowly, his voice so low she strained to hear it. "I'm sorry you have to be a part of this." Her eyes flew to his face, meeting a cold gaze. What the hell?

"Give me one reason I shouldn't kill you too," he continued, watching her closely. "I'm here for Edgar, and I hardly figured he'd have a piece like you around. What should I do with you?"

Her heart seemed to stop beating.

"I don't even know this guy," she whispered. "Just let me go. I won't tell anyone anything. I don't want to be a part of this."

"How stupid do you think I am?" he asked softly, eyes slipping down her still form. "You'll scream bloody murder if I let you go. You'll have to, or they might pin his death on you. In fact, I think I like that idea. You're a masseuse, right? I thought guys had to go to special parlors to find women like you. A call girl is the perfect murder suspect."

His mouth twisted, giving the word *masseuse* an ugly connotation. She stiffened.

"I'm a licensed massage therapist," she said. "I went to school for a long time to learn my craft, and I've helped heal a lot of suffering people."

"Shut up, bitch, nobody cares," Edgar muttered. "Sean, you don't have to kill anyone. I'm willing to work with you. We can make things right between us."

"It's too late for you, Edgar," Sean said. "I'm touched by your concern for your girlfriend, though."

"I'm not his girlfriend," Sandra said firmly. She edged slowly into the room, trying to control the shaking of her legs. Sean stepped toward her, eyes trailing across her body once more.

"I could use some of that *licensed healing*," he said, the words sounding dirty. He dropped one hand slowly to his crotch and cupped himself. Her eyes followed his hand, noticing a large, long ridge beneath his pants. Edgar shot her a glance and sidled to one side of the room. Maybe he had an idea? Not likely, but she couldn't bring herself to give him away by following him with her eyes.

"Are you going to kill me?" she asked, letting her voice go soft. She straightened her shoulders, pushing her breasts out. If Edgar needed a distraction to help rescue them, she was ready and willing to help out. Thankfully her T-shirt had a scoop neckline. Now if only she had some more cleavage . . .

"Not right away," Sean murmured, running his hand slowly up and down the length of his erection. Out of the corner of her eye she saw Edgar slip through the door. What was he doing? He was supposed to thump the bad guy over the head while she distracted him, not run away. "Not before I'm done with you. I haven't had a woman in a hell of a long time. You look just like a ripe peach to me, all soft and filled with juices."

A bolt of lightning flashed, followed by a loud clap of thunder. Edgar bolted down the hallway.

"Edgar, you bastard!" she screamed. Sean spun around, giving out a mighty bellow of anger. Sandra looked around desperately for some kind of weapon. The closest thing she could see was a wooden chair. She picked it up and brought it crashing down across the back of his head. He staggered to one side and she pushed past him out the door. She could hear his muttered curses as she ran down the hall, through the living room that masqueraded as a waiting room, and out the front door. There was no sign of Edgar. She jetted across the wet pavement toward her aging hatchback and fumbled in her jeans pocket for the keys. Where were they?

Fuck.

She'd left them inside.

A noise came from behind; he was coming. She needed to get *away*.

She took off down the street, passing boarded-up houses and small closed businesses. Nine at night, and the entire block had shut down. Why had she agreed to an evening appointment in this part of town? It was a cesspit, dangerous for a woman alone.

She could hear his footsteps thudding behind her. Damn, he was fast.

Lightning flashed again. Rain burst from the sky, hitting the pavement in splatters. Within seconds she felt it soaking her hair and her T-shirt. She slipped and almost went down, but managed to flail her arms and pull herself back upright.

He was gaining on her. She wouldn't be able to outrun him.

She turned a corner and a light called to her from a storefront diner. She put forth an extra burst of speed and started toward it. Not fast enough. His fingers caught the back of her T-shirt, ripping at it viciously. She almost went down, but she managed to keep on her feet, somehow tried to keep moving. Maybe she could rip the shirt and get away . . .

He jerked back on the fabric. Hard. She choked, falling backward, hitting the ground with such force that she couldn't breathe. He rolled onto her, roughly covering her mouth with his hand.

"You aren't getting away just yet, little girl," he said, his voice low and menacing. "I've worked too hard for this to let you fuck it up. Edgar will keep his mouth shut, he'll be too scared not to. You're another story."

Oh, she was scared all right. She choked back a sob, wishing desperately that she hadn't taken the appointment. What had she been thinking?

He lay on top of her for several tense seconds as her pulse pounded in her ears. Her chest heaved against his, the hard points of her nipples flattened against his muscles. Nothing about him gave even an inch of space. She opened her mouth, gasping against his hand for air. She couldn't get a deep breath. One small part of her mind registered he wasn't breathing hard at all. Bastard.

"I'm going to let you up slowly," he whispered in her ear. His breath was hot, menacing. "You need to keep your mouth shut. If you don't, I'll kill you. If you do exactly what I say, you may have a chance to live. Do you understand?"

She nodded her head, her gaze darting toward the diner. Why didn't anyone see her? Sure, it was dark and wet, but they were right in the middle of the street. Didn't anyone realize she needed help?

"Look at me," he said. "Convince me that you understand."

She turned her eyes toward him, getting a good look at the man for the first time. Pale blue eyes met her gaze, so pale they seemed unnatural. *Witch eyes*, she thought, shuddering. They bored through her without a trace of warmth, two orbs of ice penetrating her soul.

"Are you going to make any noise?" he asked slowly.

She shook her head as well as she could, meaning it. She had no doubt that he'd kill her if she didn't obey. *Not that he'd enjoy it,* she thought. Killing her would be no more than swatting a fly to him. He wouldn't think twice about it.

"You keep quiet and stay next to me," he said. "If we run into anyone, you agree with everything I say."

She nodded, and then he leaned up on one arm. The movement pushed his hips down into her, and to her horror she felt something press against her. That same bulge she'd seen before, only much bigger. He wanted her.

Her startled gaze flew to his face again.

"If you're good, I'll keep you around for a while," he said slowly. "You might have all kinds of uses."

With that he let her go, pushing himself to his feet and then pulling her up roughly beside him. He grabbed her upper arm and marched her down the street toward Edgar's office. As they walked, a van pulled up next to them, and for one shining moment hope filled her heart. Then the door slid open, and a black man with eyes as dead as her captor's looked at them.

"Who the hell is she?" he asked.

"She's my new toy," the man said. "She fucked up my little visit with Eddie-boy, and now she's seen too much."

"Why is she still alive?" the man asked as casually as if they were discussing a sick plant. "Valzar isn't going to like this."

"Why do you *think* she's still alive? Look at her," Sean replied, jerking his head in the general direction of her breasts. "I could use the services of a pro right now, and she's feeling motivated to stay alive. We'll work something out."

The man shrugged, apparently indifferent to her fate.

"So long as she can't ID us when this is all over," he said. "Oh, we got Edgar for you. He's in a Dumpster about a block the other direction."

"Thanks."

Sean pushed her into the van and hopped up after her. She lurched against the other man, and he pushed her back into a seat. His touch held no kindness.

"Let's go," Sean said, thumping the back of the seat before him. The van swerved out into the street, tires squealing across the wet pavement. Sandra sank back into the seat, wishing with all her might that Sean and his friends had gotten to Edgar long before she'd ever heard of the asshole.

TWO

*S*EAN COLLAPSED ON THE seat next to the hooker. He was exhausted, soaked and had missed out on getting personal revenge against the man he hated more than anyone on earth. He'd waited years for that revenge. It was revenge for his fallen men too, although they would never know about it. They had died to feed Williams's greed, along with the hostage they were trying to rescue.

Now he wanted to howl, to punch out with his fists and kill. He forced the feelings back, maintaining his frozen exterior. He had to stay calm, had to escape. Because of her, he'd lost the chance to kill Williams. He wanted to hate her, but she smelled too good, even wet and muddy. It had been five years, two months and ten days since he'd touched a woman.

He wanted desperately to touch this one.

His old friend Del sat in the seat next to them, carefully ignoring their guest. His silence spoke volumes. She was a liability, she could link all of them to Williams. He should have killed her.

Del was right, of course. She *was* a liability. He really couldn't afford to let her live, but he'd be damned if he wanted to kill her just yet. Or at all, really. A pro like her would understand, they would come to an arrangement, he told himself. Hell, she might like South America. He sure did.

He reached between his legs, adjusting his pants to a more comfortable position. His cock throbbed. He could almost feel her squirming beneath him on the ground, feel her soft breasts pushing against his chest as she gasped for air. Her belly had given way to him so easily, and he knew instinctively that her legs would have cradled him to perfection. She was a whore—she *knew* how to touch a man in all the right places. He couldn't wait to get his hands on her.

She shivered beside him. Probably cold, he thought, and scared. Sean wrapped one arm around her shoulder, pulling her stiff body against his. She didn't want to be touched—he could feel the fear radiating from her. But she was so soft and small next to him, like a little rabbit. He wanted to squeeze her. Sean lifted her onto his lap, pulling her head to his chest.

"We'll work something out," he repeated softly, trying to calm her fears.

Beside him Del gave a snort of disgust.

"You can sit up front if you like," Sean said, giving Del a pointed look. Del shook his head slowly, but leveraged his large frame up. He stood, bracing himself against the seat backs as he moved forward and dropped down into the broad passenger-side chair.

Sean ignored him, turning back to his newfound treasure instead.

Her little ass was tight and warm against him, and he could feel himself swelling even larger. He closed his eyes, and his hands clutched her body almost spasmodically. Hot. Female. His.

She moaned and gave a whimper of protest.

"Don't worry, I'll be a better customer than Edgar Williams," he said, not wanting to think about those fat hands touching her. It was better to imagine she wasn't a whore, that she was his woman, and he could do whatever he wanted with her. Of course, he *could* do whatever he wanted with her, he reflected, so long as he paid her enough. Once upon a time, the thought might have bothered him, perhaps even disgusted him.

Now it just made him harder.

He knew they'd arrive at the airstrip soon, but he couldn't help himself. He had to touch her. He grasped her small waist, lifting her and repositioning her so that she straddled his lap, facing him. He lifted his hips, pressing his erection up into the juncture of her thighs.

Damn, that was good.

She moaned once more, and he opened his eyes to look at her face.

Her eyes were large and brown in her face, pixie eyes, he thought with bitter bemusement. Not the kind of eyes you should find on a working girl. She had pale skin with a smattering of freckles across her nose, and she bit her lip nervously as she searched his face. The gesture drew his attention to her lips, and he studied them thoughtfully. They were full, slightly chapped. He imagined kissing them, knowing full well she'd probably bite him if he tried. At least he hoped she would. He liked a woman with a little spark. She didn't seem to have much fight left in her at the moment, but she'd sure given him a run for his money earlier. He'd actually thought for a moment that she might get away from him.

He wondered what she was thinking, and then decided he didn't care. She was sexy as hell. He looked lower and realized that if they had more light he'd probably be able to see right through her wet shirt. As it was, he could see the faint outline of her bra. It must be black, he realized, to stand out like that. He closed his eyes, imagining her rounded, pouty breasts draped in wisps of black lace. He groaned and rocked her forward over his cock.

He didn't want to think about how many men she'd had. He wanted to think about the soft, warm spot between her legs. He wanted to thrust up into her so hard she screamed. He imagined doing it, and his hips bucked up at her again. The friction of their clothes rubbing felt almost painful to his sensitive flesh, but he couldn't seem to stop himself. Grasping her hips firmly in his hands, he lifted her slightly and then rubbed her down the length of his cock. He did it again, repeating the motion until he thought he'd die. Tension spiraled down toward his groin, building with each motion until he thought he might burst right out of his pants.

Or worse yet, burst in them.

He reached down, determined to free his length from the imprisoning cloth. She could touch him, wrap her fingers around him and massage him right there. It would be amazing, the most perfect sensation he could imagine.

Let her earn her keep, they all had to do their part.

But even as he wormed his hand between them, the van came to a stop and Del turned to look at him with a toothy, humorless grin.

"You're lucky," he said, "Valzar's come up in the world. He's got a private jet with a bedroom. I suggest you wait until you're onboard before doing anything else. We're not out of the woods yet, you know."

Sean nodded, knowing Del was right. He'd already wasted precious time hunting Williams. His deal for protection and cover from the CIA wasn't worth a damn if he didn't even make it out of the country. The locals were still trying to catch him. Hell, he was kind of surprised they weren't waiting for him at the airstrip.

For once, though, his luck seemed to be holding. The door on the side of the van slid open, and a dark-skinned man in a loose shirt and jeans smiled at him.

"I see you haven't changed, *amigo*," Valzar said in his soft, lightly accented voice. "Always a girl in tow. Let's board the plane—we've been waiting for you. It hasn't occurred to your stupid *gringo* prison guards to shut down the airspace around here, but they'll figure it out soon enough. Let's leave before they think of it."

Sean smiled, unexpectedly pleased to see Valzar. Damn, he'd missed the man.

"Out," he said, pushing the woman off his lap and ahead of him before he jumped down onto the tarmac. In the distance he could see Valzar's plane—small, sleek and fast.

"You've come up in the world, friend," he said, giving the man a hug. The woman stood next to them awkwardly, he didn't bother watching her. Del eyed her coldly, fingering his gun.

Valzar took his arm and started walking him toward the plane. Del followed, pushing the woman along beside them. His little bird wouldn't get away while Del stood guard.

"You're a lucky man, Sean," Valzar said. "Deals like this one don't come along very often. We all thought you were long lost."

"I thought I might be too," Sean said. He'd been out of his prison cell less than four hours, but already it seemed like some kind of horrible dream.

He'd rather die than go back.

"How much do I owe you?" he asked, nodding toward the plane. "I know you must have paid them to help me escape, not to mention the tab for that little beauty."

"When I heard that an opportunity was coming, I couldn't resist," Valzar said, shrugging with Latin elegance. "Don't worry about the money. We're partners, remember? You still have plenty of cash lying around, you know. I've been taking good care of it for you."

"I didn't expect that," Sean said, shaking his head. "We always said that if one of us got caught, the other shouldn't look back. That was the plan."

"Fuck the plan," Valzar said, grinning broadly. "I enjoyed tricking the *gringo* prison guards. It was worth it just to see their stupid pig faces on the television set while we waited. They still have no idea what hit them."

"How many men escaped?" Sean asked.

"Couple hundred?" Valzar said, giving another fluid shrug. "They probably aren't even sure that you're gone yet. There's still plenty of confusion at the prison. They're rioting, you know."

"How did you arrange that?" Sean asked, almost afraid to hear the answer. Valzar had always been ruthless when it came to getting what he wanted.

"I didn't have to," Valzar said. "Our mutual friends took care of everything. All they want in return is some consideration down the line, which I was planning to give them anyway."

Sean nodded, not wanting the details. The less he knew about CIA operations, the better.

"How long will it take us to get out of U.S. airspace?" he asked. "Will that be a problem?"

"You've been in prison a long time, *amigo*," Valzar said, flashing his playboy grin. "I guess you haven't heard. I have diplomatic immunity now. This plane belongs to my government. If they try to stop us, they'll create an international incident."

THREE

*S*ANDRA WATCHED CLOSELY AS the two men walked
ahead of her, talking in what seemed like friendly
enough tones. Del marched next to her, face sullen.
Her eyes darted around, looking for ways to escape. The rain was
falling harder now, and she wondered for a moment if it would be
too dangerous for the plane to take off.

Of course not, she realized in disgust. These were men who
weren't afraid to commit murder and kidnapping. Why would
they let the weather stop them?

Of course, the weather might serve her purpose. If she found
just the right moment to break away, the darkness might provide
enough cover to escape. She stole a look at Del, who seemed to
be ignoring her. Lightning flashed again, and a thunderclap hit so
hard the very ground seemed to shake beneath their feet. It was
her shot.

She took off running as fast as she could, deliberately heading for the darkness along the side of the runway. There were no
buildings there, only a few lonely crop dusters tethered with worn
ropes. Beyond them were trees and cover. If she could just make it
that far she'd at least have a chance to escape.

She heard Del shouting behind her. It took him a couple seconds to register her escape, and then something made a cracking noise.

Shots.

Holy Mother, he was shooting his gun at her! She'd thought she was already going as fast she could, but suddenly she found more speed. The noise cracked again, and then once more. She heard more shouts from behind, and then a thudding sound. Holes appeared in one of the planes ahead of her and she gulped, terrified. She made it past the first of the planes, ducking behind it and pausing for a moment to catch her breath and clutch her side.

Big mistake.

Her captor, the one they called Sean, was right behind her, all but plowing her over when he came barreling around the plane. She lurched away from him and took off again, ignoring the terrible stitch in her side. Why hadn't she signed up for that aerobics class? She'd been meaning to do it for weeks now. Mom had been right, laziness really *would* be the death of her.

The pavement beneath her feet abruptly disappeared, and her feet sank into sandy gravel. It threw her off and she fell forward, hard, hands hitting the ground with enough force to tear off the skin. She heard him coming. She crawled forward, trying to push herself to her feet. Moving was hard, she'd knocked the breath right out of her lungs when she fell.

He hit her with the force of a train, slamming her into the ground as he came down. He was hard, wet, angry, and for one moment she wondered if he'd kill her right on the spot. Instead he just held her there, panting hard and muttering under his breath.

"That was stupid, girl," he said roughly. "Very stupid. You made me look bad in front of my friends and they aren't the kind of people to forget something like that. Neither am I, for that matter. You'll be sorry you did this."

She had no doubt he told the truth. She was sorry already. Her legs were already cramping, and she knew she'd ache in the morning. If she survived to see the morning.

"I'll do what you say," she muttered quickly. "Please don't kill me. All I want is to live. Please."

"Oh, you'll live," he said, his voice rough. "After the hassle you've given me, I'll be damned if I'll let you go this easy. You owe me now."

She didn't respond to the patently illogical statement, knowing that arguing with him was foolish. If he said she was the problem, she'd accept responsibility. Whatever it took to keep him happy was good enough for her. He pushed himself up slowly and reached one hand down to her. She took it with resignation; she was beat. Whatever chances she might have to get away were over for the moment. Now she needed to conserve her strength.

He pulled her to her feet and marched her along next to him, one hand wrapped firmly around her upper arm. It hurt and she knew she'd have bruises there the next day. Then again, she'd probably have bruises all over.

They walked in silence back through the parked planes. Del sat on the tarmac near the jet, clutching his jaw and giving her a look of such hatred that she shivered. How had he gotten hurt? The other man, Valzar, watched her with cool speculation in his eyes, as if she were some sort of strange and exotic bird he was considering eating.

She didn't like that look at all.

Sean stayed silent, marching her past both of them toward the jet. She was freezing cold now and covered in mud, but nobody seemed

to notice or care. They reached the foot of a small flight of steps
leading to the open hatch of the jet. Sean pushed her up ahead of
him, and she stumbled. One of her shoes was gone, she realized.
She was walking half barefoot through the rain and she hadn't
even noticed. Her toe throbbed, and she wondered if she was
bleeding.

They entered the plane and he pushed her toward the back.
Along each side were comfortable loungers. Nobody was in them.
He kept her moving until they reached the end of the aisle, where
a narrow door awaited them.

"Through that door," he said roughly. "We'll be able to get
cleaned up in there. I'm sure Valzar doesn't want us getting mud
all over his pretty airplane."

She opened the door to find in a surprisingly spacious room.
A large bed stood against one wall, as well as several chairs and
a closet. Another door, just past the bed, seemed to lead into a
bathroom.

"We'll shower in there later," he said coolly, letting go of her
arm for the first time. "We'll be taking off in a couple minutes, and
until we're in the air, we shouldn't be moving around the cabin.
Take off your clothes."

She stood frozen, unable to process his words.

"I said take off your clothes," he said again, opening the buttons of his own shirt. His fingers revealed a well-muscled chest
covered in springy black hair. It was broad and finely muscled. She
gaped at him, hardly believing this was real. Was he going to rape
her like this? It seemed so . . . *sudden*. She shook her head, trying
to clear her thoughts.

"Do you want me to take off your clothes for you?" he asked
coldly. "I don't want you getting mud all over the plane, and you'll
do that if you don't get that stuff off right now."

"Oh," she said, turning away and blushing. She started pull-ing the shirt over her head, and then froze. He'd stopped moving behind her. She turned to find him watching her.

"Take them off."

She pulled her wet T-shirt up slowly, wishing desperately that she'd worn a plain white bra. Why had she gone with black that morning? What had she been thinking? The shirt was gone all too soon, and she reached down to unzip her jeans.

They were soaking wet, and the zipper stuck.

She turned away from him once more, working at it and feel-ing her breath come in short puffs. Then she felt the warmth of his body behind her, and she froze. His hands reached around her, grasping the zipper in firm fingers. He worked it down slowly, and then reached his hands into the waist of her jeans to slide them down. His touch was almost gentle, a complete contrast with his tone of voice. She felt fingers graze her flesh as he pushed the wet fabric lower, across her hip bones and down the sides of her thighs. The jeans clung to her, but he slid them down with the same strength he'd used to capture her earlier. She had no doubt in that moment that he'd be able to rip them off if he wanted.

As her jeans moved lower, he knelt behind her. She felt his hot breath on her back as he dropped down, could feel the start of surprise he gave as her red thong panties came into view.

Oh Lord. She'd only worn them because she needed to do laundry. They'd been a gift from Matt, the idiot who'd dumped her two months ago for a grad student. He'd said she bored him. Oh, to go back to those boring days again . . . And to think she used to wish for a little more excitement in her life!

Sean stopped moving as the thong came into view, his breath hitting the small of her back in short, sharp puffs. He was seeing her bare ass in a way only a lover should see it, she thought miserably. Then he started moving again, sliding his hand within the jeans down to her knees.

"You can get it from here," he said roughly. She nodded, unsure of what to say, waiting for him to step back.

He didn't move.

She tried to kick her feet free of the fabric but she kept getting tangled. With a sinking feeling, she realized she was going to have to bend over and pull the jeans off. She did so slowly, wondering if the blush she could feel in her face extended all the way down her body. He had to be getting quite the view of her ass. Matt had always said it was her best feature, usually in conjunction with some kind of a comment about how her brains weren't worth a damn. Sean didn't say anything, though. He didn't touch her either, and then she was free from the heavy fabric. She stepped forward and turned slowly to face him.

"What now?" she asked, afraid to hear the answer. From the feel of his erection earlier, she had a pretty good idea what his plans were. She thought about fighting him, refusing his touch, but dismissed the idea with frightening ease. She wanted to live. If that meant accommodating him sexually, so be it. She wasn't some shrinking Victorian flower, she knew what it meant to do *it*. Hell, it couldn't be worse than Matt's drunken caresses and stinking breath.

"Get in the bed," he said, jerking his head in that direction. "You're freezing and you need to warm up. It's the best we can do for now."

"What about the sheets, won't they get wet?" she asked, and then wondered why she bothered. This was a kidnapping, not a decorating show. To hell with the sheets.

"They'll be fine," he said in a bemused tone of voice, apparently sharing her thoughts. "We can change them later. Right now I just want to get warmed up."

She turned away from him and walked slowly toward the bed. They would have sex now, she was certain of it. Maybe she could make a break past him and run out the door?

The plane's engines powered up, and she heard a thudding noise. The doors had closed. Too late. They would land eventually— she'd try to escape then. The key was to stay alive long enough to take advantage of whatever opportunities might come down the line. Staying alive meant sex.

"Come on, move," he said roughly. "We'll be taking off soon, and I don't want you to get hurt."

She smothered an absurdly inappropriate laugh, and climbed into the bed before pulling the sheets and covers up around her. The fabric was slippery and very smooth. Any other time she might have taken a moment to simply enjoy the texture of the silk, but not now. He walked across the tiny cabin all too quickly, pulling off his shirt as he moved. He stood beside the bed and unzipped his pants slowly, watching her with an intensity that frightened her. She tried not to watch, tried not to see those fingers pull down the zipper slowly and steadily, but she couldn't help herself.

He was so finely built that at any other time she'd probably be breathless by now. He was the kind of guy who never looked at women like her. Six-pack abs, a tight waist. . . . For a moment her breath caught, and she was overwhelmed with sheer appreciation for his figure.

Then he started pulling his pants down.

He wasn't wearing any underwear.

Nothing.

His penis sprang into view, fully erect and pulsing with dark red arousal. He dropped the pants down, kicked them off, then leaned over the bed. His face lowered toward hers, and he whispered in her ear.

"I won't hurt you, but you have to accommodate me," he said softly. "I've been without a woman for a long, long time, and if I don't feel you next to me pretty soon, I'm going to die. Understand?"

She nodded her head, although she wasn't quite sure what he meant by "accommodate." For all she knew he was some sick bastard who got off on telling women they were safe and then killing them.

She wanted to believe him, though. Desperately.

He pulled the covers down and slowly slid in next to her. The plane lurched, and she felt panic rising in her chest. He was too close to her, his heat was all around her and she could smell him. Slightly sweaty, male, damp.

She couldn't take it anymore. Throwing off the covers, she tried to roll out of the bed. He was on her in a flash, pulling her into his arms and wrapping his legs around hers. She struggled for a moment then fell limp against him.

His naked cock pulsed against the flesh of her stomach. Groaning, he pumped his hips into her softness and she gave a little moan of fright.

"Don't tempt me too much," he said tightly. "I don't want to hurt you, but I can't guarantee what I'll do if you keep wiggling around like that."

She froze. The heat of his erection burned through her. It was too much.

"Why are you doing this to me?" she asked with a panicky voice. "I don't deserve this. I was just doing my job."

It seemed to be the wrong question.

"Funny, I was just doing my job too, and I ended up in jail for five years," he muttered. "Do you know what it feels like to go without fucking for five years? I want to slam into you so hard it makes my head hurt. Do what I say, and that won't happen to you. At least not tonight."

Had she heard him right? Everything was happening so fast, it felt like she was spinning.

"What do you want me to do?" she asked. "Tell me exactly what I can to do keep you happy."

"For one thing, I want you to lie in this damn bed and stop trying to run away," he said, loosening his hold on her. He didn't let her go completely, but he no longer squeezed her.

"I want you to hold me and make me come. It doesn't have to be in your prissy little body, although why you're so uptight, I don't understand. If you can let Edgar fuck you, I sure as shit don't understand why you don't let me."

His harsh words cut through her, and she had to hold back a sniff. She felt like crying. *Don't be a wimp*, she told herself sharply. *Be strong, be brave. Survive and move forward.*

"I can touch you," she said slowly. "Will you let me move?"

He held her for a moment longer, then let her slide out of his arms.

"Can we turn the light off?" she asked, looking around the brightly lit cabin with distaste.

"So you can pretend I'm someone else?" he asked, his face twisted with dark humor. "I don't care if you imagine that, but I do want to see you. It's been too long for me."

She nodded and looked around again. What was she supposed to do?

"You can start by touching me," he said, as if reading her mind. "Rub my chest."

She reached out with one hand, laying her fingers flat between his nipples. The plane shuddered again, they were starting their taxi down the runway.

"Is it safe to fly like this?" she asked hesitantly.

"Well, it's against FAA regulations to fly without a seat belt," he said in a low voice. "But I'm relatively certain they won't be inspecting us, so don't worry about it."

Her breath caught, and she realized he'd made a joke. What kind of kidnapper made jokes?

"What if we hit turbulence?" she asked.

"I'll hold you," he said. "Trust me, I'd enjoy it. Now do your thing."

She moved her hand lightly on his chest, unsure of what should come next. He gave her a look of impatience, then grabbed her hand and pulled it over his right nipple.

"Let your hand drift back and forth," he said. "Play with it. And smile while you're doing it."

She did as her told her, allowing her fingers to brush back and forth across his taut skin. The nipple was hard and nubby, and as she let her fingers graze across it, she could see goose bumps rising on his flesh.

She kept moving her hand as his head fell back and his eyes closed. The plane stopped, and then the engines started making a different noise. Louder. They were going to take off. No sooner had she thought it than the plane started moving again. They were going very fast, and the force of their acceleration pushed her down into the bed. He reached out and took her into his arms once more, anchoring her.

"I don't want you falling out of bed and hurting yourself," he said, and she felt absurdly grateful for the small comfort. She could tell the instant they left the ground, felt the pull of gravity that crushed her into his embrace. The entire cabin tilted sharply and they were in the air. He pulled her more closely into his arms, turning her to face him. His legs tangled with hers, and his hands reached down to cup her bottom. Without understanding quite how it happened, she suddenly found his cock slipping between her legs. It pressed at the entrance to her womb, but the sheer fabric of her panties kept him out.

"I thought you weren't going to come in me," she gasped, trying to pull away. The plane lurched, throwing her onto him. He rolled onto his back, taking her with him.

"Touch me," he muttered, his voice harsh. "Touch me and I won't come in you."

She reached a hand down, worming it in between them. Her earlier shyness melted away. She wanted to touch him, to get him off as fast as she could. She didn't think those scraps of red lace would keep him out much longer. Her knees slipped to either side of his hips, supporting her as she raised her pelvis.

He pulled his body back from hers a bit as she reached down, giving her access to his groin. Her hand found his penis. It was long, hard and smooth. She wrapped her fingers around it, her grasp slipping from the moisture leaking from his tip. *It's just another way to give a massage,* she told herself, knowing it was a blatant lie.

This was no legitimate massage.

He gasped as her fingers took him firmly, and she slid her hand down his length slowly. His entire body was rigid and hard, a study in tension and arousal.

"Again," he muttered. She did as he said, looking up at his face while she did. His eyes closed, his head tilted back. The cords in his neck were taut, and she realized just how much control it was taking for him not to move. She slid her hand down his shaft again, and felt hope for the first time. He seemed almost concerned for her comfort.

His cock was stiff, quivering beneath her hand.

"That's just right," he whispered, and her breath caught. His voice was low, husky, and filled with a longing that gave her chills. A twinge of sensation caught her between her thighs, and her nipples peaked beneath the black bra.

Oh, this just kept getting more and more complicated.

FOUR

ER TOUCH WAS ALMOST more than he could bear.

Five long years he'd spent imagining what it would be like to have a woman's hand on his body. Years spent closing his eyes, lying back on his bunk and stroking himself when he could bear the loneliness no longer.

Five years of hatred and waiting, lifting weights in the yard and plotting his escape.

Five years knowing everything he'd worked so hard for could be stolen at any moment.

It overwhelmed him.

He suddenly thrust against her hand powerfully. She gasped. Skittish as all hell, and afraid too. He knew he should care, knew he shouldn't take her, but he'd be damned if he'd stop now. Taking care of men like him was her job. She might say she wasn't that kind of masseuse, but he knew better. Williams wasn't the kind of man who would go for a straight massage. Her nimble fingers slid up and down his cock, cupping and squeezing him in a way that made him want to explode on the spot. Back and forth across his flesh, skin tightening with every motion.

He shifted, trying not to imagine what it would feel like to push her back, thrust his knee between her legs and fuck her hard. *She's a whore, she expects it,* his cock whispered greedily. *Don't push her too hard,* his brain cautioned. *She'll break.*

Her fingers came closer and closer to the head of his cock with every stroke. The little ridge of skin that defined it twitched as she edged toward it, then her fingers grazed his most sensitive spot.

"Not there," he muttered, and she stilled. "If you touch me there I'll come off like a rocket, and I want to enjoy this a little longer."

She started moving again and he made himself focus on more than just the feel of her hot skin rubbing him. The smell of her hair, wet with just a trace of floral scent. Shampoo?

It was better than any perfume he'd imagined in the joint.

Her breasts formed taut peaks against his chest as if aroused, burning into him like hot pokers. He knew it was probably from the cold, but that didn't matter to his hungry body. If only she were wet for him too. His hand reached down automatically, he wanted to check. He felt her breath catch as she realized what he was doing and he stopped.

He wasn't going to touch her there. If he touched her, he'd fuck her. He didn't want her screaming and crying, didn't want to hurt her.

So instead he forced his hand back, took a deep breath and spoke.

"You can start moving again," he said gruffly.

Her fingers flexed around his taut flesh and he grunted. The tension in his body leapt back to where it'd been just seconds before, he wasn't going to last long. Her strong hand moved up and down, and without thinking he pushed against her. Her fingers tightened again, and she squeezed him. He thrust once more, and this time her fingers squeezed in time with his movements.

They fell into a rhythm, his hips thrusting and her fingers caressing him. The blood sped through his body, pounding in his ears, making his breathing grow harsh.

Tension curled inward in his body and he grew harder. His balls tightened, gathering for his release, and then he exploded in her hand. His seed blew out with explosive force and he grunted, thrusting into her hand as she pumped him dry. For one second darkness took over his vision, the sheer animal pleasure of his orgasm more than he could comprehend. He lay there, sucking air into his lungs and sweating, for what seemed like eternity. She stayed next to him, frozen, her hand still cupping his softening cock. For a moment he wondered if she was trying to harden him again, but then he realized the truth.

She was afraid to move her hand without permission.

"You can let go," he grunted. She pulled away instantly, rolling as far away from him across the bed as she could.

Absently, he noted that the plane had leveled off.

"We can take a shower now," he said, and he heard her breath catch.

"Together?" she asked breathlessly.

"No, you can go by yourself," he said slowly. An image of her body dripping with warm water entered his head and he almost moaned aloud.

She'd only taken the edge off so far.

"Alone," he replied. "But don't take a long time. I might change my mind."

"I'll go fast," she said, voice fervent. She rolled out of the bed, trying to take the sheet with her as a cover.

"Leave it," he said shortly. Watching her was half the joy, he wasn't going to give it up that easily.

She stood quickly and crossed her arms across her barely

covered breasts. He wondered if she had any idea how sexy she looked. Her hair hung down around her shoulders in scraggly lines, and the little red thong she wore hardly covered a thing. Her hands and the lace-bound breasts they covered were more of a taunt than anything.

He felt himself stir once more as she moved quickly past the bed to the small bathroom, lurching as she walked. The air was fairly smooth, especially considering what a storm raged outside, but he could still feel the motion of the plane around them. He heard the shower come on and imagined her in there. Her fingers were probably sticky with his seed. He'd be willing to bet she'd wash it off first, eager to remove any trace of his touch from her body. There were splashes of it on her belly as well, and he thought about her hands rubbing against the creamy flesh as she cleaned it off.

Did she have any idea how soft and smooth her skin was?

He was willing to bet she didn't.

She probably took her flesh for granted, never thinking twice about what a treat it would be for a man like him. Of course, he wouldn't have had any idea either before he went into the joint. Nobody could. He rolled onto his back, crossing his hands behind his head and looking up at the cabin ceiling. They were still over the States, but he doubted he had anything to worry about. Not in a plane like this. Trust Valzar to get appointed as a diplomat. What the hell were they thinking? That was certainly putting the fox in charge of the henhouse.

He heard the water shut off, and he smiled with bitter amusement.

She didn't want him joining her.

A moment later the door opened and she came back into the room, a white towel clutched around her body.

"I thought you might like to shower next," she said, sidling back into the room.

"You were afraid I'd come in there," he said, watching her coolly. She probably thought holding the towel tight to her body provided cover. Instead it simply teased him with her curves.

His cock stirred to life.

"Although it'd be nice if you offered to wash me," he said slowly. She froze, eyes cutting through him. "Perhaps another time. I don't want you to think I don't appreciate what you've already done for me."

She simply looked at him, eyes haunted.

He rolled out of the bed abruptly, coming to his feet in one smooth motion. She jumped back and he laughed.

"I'm just going to shower," he said, looking at her pointedly. "Trust me, when I decide to fuck you, you'll know it."

She didn't reply, and he laughed again. Her fear should have made him sick. Instead it simply awakened his hunter's instinct. He considered making her fears come true but decided against it.

There would be plenty of time when they landed.

SHE WATCHED IN A daze as he stalked into the bathroom.

When he was gone she could hardly imagine he'd been there. He was too unreal, too scary. It reminded her of the one time she'd tried drugs during college. Intense, scary, almost unbelievable when it ended. Only the pictures her friends had taken of her dancing wildly in a club were enough to convince her she'd really been that crazed girl.

Her gaze drifted across the room, coming to rest on the door. No point in trying to run. Even if they weren't in the air, that outside cabin was filled with his friends. She wasn't sure about Valzar, but she'd bet every last penny she had that Del wanted her dead, assuming he was on the plane. She had no way of knowing who might be out there. The cold reality of the situation was that as long as Sean wanted her, she was his.

It was the best way to stay alive.

She thought of the heroines in romance novels, fighting bravely to preserve their precious virginity.

Fuck that.

She'd do whatever it took to keep alive, including blowing every man on the plane.

The thought was so overwhelming that she sat down on the bed, letting the towel fall to the floor. She really was prepared to do whatever it took to stay alive. It was as if a switch flipped within her head. Suddenly she felt lighter, freer. The old inhibitions fell away as everything stood out in her mind with stark clarity.

Staying alive was all that mattered.

The shower stopped running as a burst of turbulence hit the plane. He gave a muffled grunt from the bathroom, and she fell back on the bed, bemused. He was strong, and the other men respected him. Even Valzar, their leader, listened to him. As long as she kept him happy, he would protect her. Eventually she'd find a way to escape. All she had to do was make him want her . . .

He came out of the bathroom. Mentally she poured herself a shot of vodka, drank it back and sat up.

"We didn't exactly finish before, did we?" she asked, hoping her voice was sultry and sophisticated. He froze, eyes searching her face. A slow, curious smile came over his features.

"No, I guess we didn't finish," he said.

Sandra sat back, spreading her legs across the silk sheets. Her breasts thrust forward as she leaned back on her hands.

"I think we need to come to an understanding," she said softly.

"I don't know what's going on here and I don't care. All I care about is me. If you take good care of me, I'll take very good care of you."

He didn't react at first, and she flushed nervously. Would he notice? She hoped not. She wanted him to see her as a sophisticated woman of the world. If he took her offer at face value, he'd be less careful.

"I suppose we could do that," he said slowly. "Although I think we should make things clear from the start. It sounds to me like you're a professional?"

"Yes," she said, hoping her smile wasn't slipping. "You were right about that before. I'm a professional, and I don't make it my business to pry into the personal affairs of the men I serve."

"So why weren't you more accommodating before?" he asked softly.

"Because you startled me," she said, trying to look up at him through her eyelashes. "Even a professional can get spooked when her new client tries to kill her old client."

His face grew thoughtful, and she bit the inside of her lip. She shouldn't have reminded him that she knew about the murder. Big mistake.

"Enough about that," she said quickly. Pushing herself forward, she stood and strolled slowly toward him. "Why don't you turn those lights down and come over here?" she asked softly. "I like to work with my hands, and you strike me as being very . . . tense."

He watched her without moving, and she thought he'd seen through her for sure. Then he turned and walked across the room to the light switch and turned it off. A dim glow—emergency lights?—came from the corners of the room. Not bright enough to keep a person from sleeping, but enough that she could see the outline of his form as he came toward her.

Lord, he was big.

His bulk came from muscles too. She realized with a start that if he really *was* a client of hers, she'd be thrilled. There was nothing she loved more than going to work on a body that was well put together. She could tell just from watching him move where his trouble spots would be: Tension in the shoulders, of course, and perhaps in the lower arms. His thighs. There would be tension there too, although not the kind she could easily massage away. She backed slowly around the bed, beckoning him to follow her. Instead, he crawled onto the silken sheets like some great predatory cat. She met him halfway across the bed with a smile. He reached for her, but she raised one hand and planted it in the middle of his chest.

"This is what I do best," she said firmly. "Let me do my work and I'll guarantee you won't regret it."

He hesitated before allowed her to roll him onto his belly.

She knelt beside him and closed her eyes, formulating her strategy. He was just like any other massage client, she reminded herself. The only difference was that this massage would be more sensual.

She knew how to do it.

She'd had dreams about giving a massage like this, private fantasies about taking one of her clients and changing his entire worldview in an hour. She couldn't *do* such a thing, of course, even if she had a client she wanted to do it *to*. It wasn't right, it wasn't professional.

Professional ethics hadn't been created for situations like this, however.

She stretched out her fingers and touched him.

His flesh was cooler than she'd expected and still slightly damp from the shower. She started at the back of his neck, slowly running her fingers down along the smooth line of his back, gaining a feel for how he was built. She'd underestimated just how muscular he was. Thank goodness she wasn't doing a deep tissue massage. It might kill her fingers to work with those muscles. After a few experimental strokes she allowed herself to move more aggressively. Not too hard yet, she was still warming him up, but hard enough that she could feel his strength.

In the darkness it was easy to imagine this was nothing more than a dream. It was easy to let her fingers wander, and before long she noticed that she wasn't following her regular routine. Rather than moving across his flesh systematically, seeking out every muscle group and testing it for tension, she found herself following his contours. She leaned over, breathing deeply of his scent. A tendril of desire whispered its way up across her spine.

She shook her head, denying it. She didn't want him; it was the fantasy.

But as she moved down his back to his tight butt, she knew it was more than fantasy. He shifted restlessly as she massaged the globes of his ass, parting his legs ever so slightly. She thought about his scrotum down there, waiting for her touch, and without thinking she let her hand drift between his legs. The skin there was smooth and soft. He moaned as her fingers danced across the tender skin. He lifted his hips slightly and she cupped the sac in her hand. His testicles, those same tight balls that had shot their seed over her just half an hour earlier, slid between her fingers. She played with them, and secretly acknowledged that she liked the power touching him made her feel.

That's what it was, she realized suddenly. This new touching gave her power, a kind of control over her situation she hadn't had before. Like millions of women before her, she could control a man using her body. It wasn't something she would normally have considered a good thing, but now it was priceless. That power could save her life.

His hips lifted ever so slightly, and she realized he was rubbing the smooth silk sheets with his penis. She removed her hand, and placed it firmly in the center of his back. She pushed him down, stilling his motion.

"All in good time," she said quietly, then traced her tongue across the small of his back. She worked her hands down the backs of his thighs, letting go of her massage technique and using feminine instinct to guide her touch. Here he was definitely tense. She could feel his arousal in every bit of skin, every wiry hair her fingers grazed. Massage wouldn't help that. She started down again, moving toward the backs of his knees. He seemed especially sensitive there. She kissed him once, twice, tracing the skin with her tongue, wiggling it back and forth to tickle him.

"No more of that," he muttered after a moment. She considered ignoring him, but stopped herself. Instinct might tell her to continue, but she wasn't so sure of her hold on him that she felt it safe to disobey. Better to do as he said. She took deep breaths for several moments and then muttered, "All right."

She started back down his legs until she reached his feet. Then she knelt at the end of the bed, taking them into her lap and rubbing first one and then the other between her strong fingers. He actually shuddered in pleasure and gave a mighty stretch. Once again she was reminded of a giant cat, something one might find in a jungle. Something that ate only that which it caught, killing without mercy. She shivered and dropped his feet.

"Why don't you roll over now?" she said, trying to keep her voice strong. She wanted to whisper, she wanted to run away, but that wasn't going to happen. She'd already dealt herself the hand she needed to win, now she just had to play it.

He did as she said, and in the dim light of the room she could see his erection jutting above his flat belly. That monster was going to be in her body. As she shook her head, trying to rid herself of the imagery, he tilted his head up at her.

"Second thoughts?" he asked with a challenge in his voice.

"No," she said, and to prove him wrong she started crawling up his body with one knee on either side of him. "I'm just getting started."

FIVE

*H*ER WORDS SENT A shiver racing down his spine.

Fuck, this was better than his fantasies in the joint. She slithered up his body so smoothly he hardly knew what hit him, and everything about her screamed *female*. His senses, already attuned to her, leapt to life and screamed at him to take her, roll her over and thrust into her body with every last bit of his strength.

Instead he stilled himself, allowing her the freedom to continue her exploration. He'd been dreaming about this moment for years. He wanted to savor her, like he'd savor a fine whiskey.

He couldn't stop himself from running his hands up her arms, though. He could feel the fine strength in her. These were the arms of a woman who worked out, who kept herself in good shape. He couldn't help admiring that about her. He cupped her breasts, squeezing them softly, flicking the nipples with his fingers. They perked up, and he looked into her eyes to see surprise there.

Apparently she wasn't used to being attracted to her clients. He felt a moment of smug satisfaction. He'd gotten through to her, whether she wanted to admit it or not.

She leaned forward, resting her weight against his hands. She straddled him, one knee resting on either side of his upper thighs, and the soft flesh of her belly brushed the head of his cock.

"Touch me there," he commanded, and she gave a low laugh. The kind of laugh only a woman in control could give. For a second he wondered if he should be concerned, but he wiped the thought away. He controlled her, whatever she might think. That was the way it would be between them.

She pulled back and took one of his hands in each of her own.

"Put these down," she said, giving him a sly smile. "I don't like to work on someone unless they're totally still."

"That must be kind of hard sometimes," he replied softly. "Do all your clients do what you say?"

"If they want me to keep them as clients," she said lightly. "I'm very picky about who I'll work on."

He rolled his eyes, but let his hands fall back as she asked. He had plenty of time to play with her. Apparently she had some kind of kinky specialty, and he might as well take advantage of it.

"Do your worst," he said, closing his eyes. An image of her strong, slender hands wrapped around his throat drifted through his mind. He shook his head, willing the image away. She didn't have half his strength, he could easily defend himself. After all, where was she going to run? They were on a plane, and there was no escape from his friends up front.

Her fingers came to rest on his chest, digging into the muscles. He tried to think back to the last time he'd been touched like this. There had been that whore two nights before he'd been caught, but she didn't have this woman's talent. She was definitely higher class than the average call girl. Although what was up with her clothing? He'd never seen a hooker dressed like that before . . .

Her fingers made their way down his chest, coming ever closer to his stomach and the jutting length of his erection. Every touch, every gentle nudge, brought him a little closer to the edge. Each time, though, she seemed to back off. Why was she so bound and determined to hold him back?

She gripped the tops of his thighs and started sliding down and away from him. This was too much.

"Enough," he said, his voice harsh with need. He sat up abruptly, reaching down and pulling her across his body. "Enough of this teasing, I want to fuck. You can stay on top or be on the bottom, I don't care."

She stilled, and for a moment her expression clouded. He almost wondered if she was going to say something, but then a strange, strained smile stole across her face.

"I'll stay on top," she said, her voice soft and thready. "I'd really rather be on top."

"Fine," he said, and pulled her hard against his chest. He fell back across the bed, grasping her head firmly in his hands. He pulled her close for a kiss, hands gripping her face so she couldn't escape, and then his mouth took hers.

She tasted sweet. Her mouth was soft, *too* soft for a whore. No woman should taste like that unless she was meant for just one man, he thought almost angrily. He pushed his tongue into her mouth forcefully, wanting to wipe away that taste of innocence. She was too sweet, too nice to touch. It wasn't right.

She sank into his kiss, and before he realized what he was doing he'd rolled her under him. His legs thrust between hers, spreading them apart. Still kissing her deeply, he drove into her, amazed at how tight she was. She gasped into his mouth, and her entire body stiffened around his. He'd hurt her, had pushed in too fast. He pulled away from the kiss and buried his head in her hair, breathing deeply.

"I'm sorry," he muttered. "It's been so long. You have no idea how good you feel."

He felt her flex her muscles around him experimentally and groaned. How was he supposed hold back when she felt like that?

"If you keep doing that, I won't be able to control myself."

She stilled, and he took several deep, harsh breaths. Blood roared in his ears, and Sean fought to slow the pounding of his heart, fought to control the need to take her. An eternity passed, then he took control again.

He pulled back, sliding out of her with a slick wetness that belied her tension. However tight she might be, she still wanted him. Her juices were flowing thick. He slowly pushed back in. It was easier this time. Following his instincts, he tilted his hips back and pulled out once more. This time he could feel himself rub against her clit as he slid home. She moaned, deep and low, and he did it again. Within moments her arms came up around him, and he felt her hips lift to meet his. He smiled into her hair, feeling pleased for some strange reason. Pro or not, she was definitely enjoying this.

He moved faster, taking deep, long breaths each time, pacing himself as he listened to her breathing. She gasped with every thrust, and he felt her legs come up around his hips to clench him close. That was more like it.

Faster and faster he moved, the pressure building up inside his body with each thrust. It was so much better than he'd remembered, falling into a woman's warm body. He had to stop several times to regain his control.

She was slick and hot now. There could be no doubt how much she wanted him. With a smile of satisfaction, he slid in and out of her body with new purpose. He was going to come soon, and he wanted her to come with him. As his flesh slapped against hers, he could feel her release start to overcome her. He moaned as little twinges deep in her body danced along his length and she started to curl up into him as if her life depended on his touch.

Then it hit her.

Her entire body went tense as her vaginal muscles gripped him with such force that it should have been painful, instead it was amazing and wonderful. He thrust again, forcing his cock past the rigid layers of muscle, each delicious touch tantalizing and torturing until he reached his limit. Sean exploded into her body.

He grunted, and his hips spasmed violently as he shot his seed. All thought ceased as pleasure rushed through him and he squeezed her until she cried out in protest. Slowly he came down, taking in deep breaths and collapsing onto her body. He felt something pushing at him, and he realized it was her hands. Why was she pushing him away?

Sean rolled off her and she turned away from him quickly. Her shoulders shuddered, and he realized she was crying. What the hell? He touched her back hesitantly, suddenly out of his realm. He liked whores because they didn't cry. Or if they did, he dismissed them. What was going on here?

She shook her head as he rubbed her shoulder, then she sat up, wiping the tears away from her face. Her skin was blotchy and her nose ran. Not pretty crying, certainly not done for effect. He opened his mouth to speak and she cut him off with one raised hand. He bit back his question, trying to figure out what to do next.

"Can we please just get some rest?" she asked softly, wiping the back of her hand across her face once more.

He nodded his head hesitantly, utterly confused. She rolled

into a small ball facing away from him, pulling up the silken sheets to her chin. Sean watched her for another moment in puzzled silence, then turned away and rolled off the bed. They had a long flight ahead of them, maybe she was right. Sleep would be good. He was far more relaxed now than he'd been in months. Safer too.

He walked across the room, allowing himself to enjoy the feeling of the plush carpet between his toes. Casually he flicked off the dim emergency lights and then returned to the bed. He hadn't lost his sense of direction in prison, he noted wryly. If anything he was even more attuned to moving without being seen after spending five years in shared cells.

He made it back to the bed and crawled in. Her crying had died down, leaving only the occasional muffled hiccup in its wake. Definitely not crying to get attention.

He lay there in the darkness for what seemed like hours until she fell asleep. Then he curled himself around her, pulling her into the circle of his arms and letting his head rest against the soft mass of her hair. Damn, she smelled good. His cock stirred in interest, but he stayed still.

There would be plenty of time to play with her more when they arrived in San Beneficio. Hopefully she'd stop crying too.

SANDRA CAME AWAKE SLOWLY, unsure of where she was. The bed was soft and comfortable, but there was a strange humming noise all around her. The floor dropped, then came back up beneath her, and she realized she must be on a plane.

But what kind of plane had a bed?

A soft snore drifted into her consciousness, startling her awake. She wasn't alone. Memories of the night before filled her mind.

She looked around the room, startled that it could be real. Where was she, and how could she escape?

She turned to look at the big man sleeping beside her. His long dark hair spilled across the pillow, hiding his face from her. She shifted, feeling sticky between her thighs.

Shit.

She'd had sex with him and they hadn't used any protection. Thoughts of HIV filled her head, followed by the thought of a black-haired baby. Or worse yet, a black-haired baby with HIV.

She clutched one hand to her stomach and moaned in horror. How had this happened to her?

He shifted and she stilled. The last thing she needed was for him to wake up. The longer he slept, the happier she'd be. Moving carefully so as not to disturb the bed, she slid out from between the sheets and walked back toward the tiny bathroom. Dark humor pierced her cloud of unhappiness as she noted that even rich people had to make do with small bathrooms on airplanes. Still, it was a very expensive plane. She had no doubt that her mysterious captor and his friends had money.

She stepped into the tiny shower and cleaned herself quickly, trying to rub herself free of the residue of his touch. She scrubbed extra hard at her breasts and between her legs, punishing her traitorous flesh for enjoying his attentions so much. When she'd decided to martyr her virtue to stay alive, she hadn't counted on enjoying it. Sean was definitely the best lover she'd ever had, and she didn't like that one bit. It wasn't fair.

Life is not fair, Sandra reminded herself as she stepped out of the shower. She pulled a plush towel out of a cupboard and dried herself off, noticing a stack of thick terry cloth bathrobes above the towels. Just what she needed. Concealing, comfortable, and utterly unsexy.

She pulled on the robe and walked back out into the bedroom. It was light outside, but the shades drawn over the windows kept things dim. She stood for a moment, waiting for her eyes to adjust. Before she could see anything, he spoke.

"Feeling better?" he asked slowly, and the sound sent a tingle rushing down her spine. Sternly she reminded herself he was the bad guy. Bad guys shouldn't have voices like that—it wasn't fair.

"Yes, thank you," she said. As her eyes adjusted she made her way over to a chair, then sat down in it as demurely as possible.

He leaned forward in the bed, covers falling to his waist, and she made herself look away.

"You want to come back to bed?" he asked. "We've still got a while before we land, and I could use another roll."

She closed her eyes against the surge of longing his words lit in her. This wasn't right.

"Do I have to?" she asked bluntly. He looked startled.

"Why should you care?" he asked. "You'll get paid, I already promised you that. I guess my promises don't mean very much to you, do they?"

She shook her head.

"I'll do what it takes to survive," she said slowly. "But I'm concerned about health and safety. We didn't use protection last night. Do you realize that I could already be pregnant? Not to mention AIDS."

He froze, peering at her closely through the darkness.

"You aren't on the Pill?" he asked quickly. "I don't have AIDS, so I'm not worried about that. Unless you have it?"

She pondered telling him she did, but figured that might set him off.

"No, I'm clean," she said slowly. "But I'm not on the Pill."

"Is that really wise for someone in your profession?"

She gave a brief, harsh laugh. She hadn't had sex since Matt, and here Sean thought she did this every day. It would be funny if it weren't so damn pathetic. She couldn't say that to him, of course. Safety lay in making him believe she was a professional who knew how to take money and keep her mouth shut.

"I prefer to use condoms," she said simply, looking down at her folded hands. "It's just always seemed a lot smarter to me. Protects against disease, you know."

He nodded his head, eyes filled with a speculative look.

"Sure," he said. "I have no problem with that."

Silence fell between them. There was a knock at the door.

"Yes?" he asked, his voice sharp and businesslike.

The door opened a crack, and Valzar stuck his head in.

"I know you're busy," he said in accented tones. "But I think you should come out and see me. I've got some good news for you."

Sean nodded and slid out of bed, apparently unconcerned by his nudity.

"Stay here," he told her with a trace of humor in his voice. "Valzar, you got any clothing in here I can use?"

"In the drawer," Valzar said, nodding his head toward the built-in dresser. "I brought some just for you. I'll be out front."

With that he closed the door behind him and the room fell silent again. Sean pulled on his clothes and left without a word.

Valzar sat in one of the large, comfortable-looking chairs, a laptop computer propped open in front of him. He looked like a businessman flying to some important meeting, but he was no ordinary businessman. Sean marveled again at his friend's ingenuity. How had he wangled diplomatic immunity?

"Good news," Valzar said, flashing Sean a grin. "Did you know you're dead?"

"Already?" Sean asked. "They move fast. How did it happen?"

"Well, according to our friends at the CIA, you stole a small plane from the airport and disappeared soon afterward. The wreckage will be found outside Fort Wiconda in about three days, and your body will be recovered. They're not too happy about the fact that you took a hostage, by the way."

"Oh, really?" Sean asked, dropping into the chair across from Valzar. "I suppose it complicates things on their end?"

"That's the gist of this message," Valzar replied with a quick smile. "Apparently they're doing some fast work to trace her and get enough information to fake her death believably. They said that it would have been a lot easier if you'd just killed her. At least then they'd have a body. I can see their point."

He shot Sean a pointed look. Sean sighed, and then closed his eyes for a moment, gathering his thoughts.

"I didn't want to kill her," he said. "There's been too much killing already, and she didn't do anything to deserve it."

"You've always been soft," Valzar said, his face growing serious. "But your little toy is going to get us in trouble. She's the only one who knows you aren't dead, and that's going to cause serious problems. You can't let her go home and you can't trust her. What are you going to do with her, keep her forever?"

Sean shook his head, knowing Valzar was right. But when he thought about closing those brown pixie eyes forever, he couldn't do it. Not now. Maybe later.

"She's my problem, not yours," he said finally. "She can't tell anyone anything as long as she's with me. You have nothing to fear from her."

Valzar nodded his head.

"That's certainly true," he said. "But I'm worried about you. I've gone to a lot of trouble to save your sorry hide, and I'd hate to see you blow it for a woman."

"I'm a big boy," Sean replied. "I can take care of her when the time comes."

SIX

HEAT PRESSED DOWN LIKE a pillow, muffling her breath.

She couldn't remember ever feeling such heat and such punishing humidity. *Thank God the car was air-conditioned,* Sandra thought grimly. Otherwise she'd be dead by now.

She and Sean sat in the backseat of a Lexus SUV, a far cry from her worn Honda. Valzar sat in the passenger seat, drumming his fingers idly against his leg. Their driver, a tall, dark-featured man with a scarred lip, drove in silence. In fact, she hadn't heard him say a single word since he'd picked them up at the airport. She hadn't seen Del.

She wanted to ask where they were going, but to judge from the looks Valzar had given her before, conversation wasn't a good idea. He seemed to take her presence as a personal insult, so instead of talking she watched out the window as they drove. She was pretty sure they were in South America. The accents and climate told her that much. They had landed on a small airstrip in the mountains. Now they were traveling through dense jungle, and she could only see the road ahead. Trees and foliage surrounded them on both sides, making the way nearly impassable.

"Almost there," Valzar said from the front seat. "You can stay as long as you like, of course. When you're ready to discuss your future and other options, let me know. I've got some ideas we can look into."

Even as he spoke, they came around a bend in the road into a clearing. Perched on a hillside before them was a white stucco-covered villa four times the size her parents' house had been. Two wings extended to either side, accented gracefully by the explosion of tropical flowers from the well-manicured bushes.

"It's paradise," she said softly, then blushed as both men turned to her. Sean smiled. Valzar's expression was more difficult to read.

"We're hundreds of miles from the nearest town," Valzar said. "This jungle is filled with animals that would love to kill and eat you. Don't think for one moment that there's any way for you to get away unless we send a plane for you."

She bit her lip and looked away. Sean nudged her and grinned.

"You'll be fine," he said. "I promised you that already."

"Don't make promises you can't keep, friend," Valzar said tightly.

They fell silent. The driver turned off the large SUV, and unlocked the doors with a click. Sean opened his and stepped out, pulling her behind him, and the heat hit her like a wall. The house seemed further away. They walked toward it quickly, but she could already feel the sweat running down her back and pooling between her breasts. It didn't help that she wore oversized men's clothing—that was all they'd had on the plane. The legs were far too long for her, and she only had one shoe. She watched her step carefully, expecting some kind of poisonous tropical bug to run out and bite her, but nothing happened.

They entered the house and another wave of cool air-conditioning washed over her. She all but moaned with pleasure. They were in a large entry hall. It held a high ceiling adorned with a giant chandelier. The floor was tiled with cool brown stones, and a broad staircase opened into the center of the room before them. Halfway up it split into two opposing staircases. They led to an open galleried second floor.

"Nice," Sean said shortly, casting a glance at Valzar. "Do I want to know who this place belongs to?"

"My family," Valzar said, sketching a short, mocking bow. "My father has always believed that wise men should have a nice, secure place to wait out a revolution. It's come in handy over the years. We have a skeleton staff here. They'll see to all your needs. They're very discreet, of course."

Someone coughed, and she noticed a man dressed in khaki pants and a white shirt standing off to one side. Valzar nodded at him, and he stepped forward.

"I'm Eduardo," he said in softly accented tones. "I run the household here, as well as being in charge of security. If you need anything at all, please just let me know."

"Thank you," Sean said.

"Eduardo has been with our family for more than twenty years," Valzar said. "He does far more for us than simply run the household."

"I understand," Sean said, and his eyes took on a new look. Sadness? It was hard to know. She could tell that something was going on here, but she had no idea what it might be.

"I trust that Eduardo isn't so zealous in doing his duty that he won't check with me before doing me any favors?" Sean asked pointedly. "I would take that as a personal insult, no matter how good the intentions were."

"I respect your right to handle your own affairs, *Señor*," Eduardo said. He shot her a look Sandra didn't like one bit. "The situation is fully under your jurisdiction. I'm simply available should you need any help."

Shit, they were talking about her. About *killing* her. She shivered and edged closer to Sean without thinking. He wrapped one arm around her, comforting her, and Valzar shot her another sharp look. She was tired of all these men looking at her, judging her. All she wanted was to go home.

"*Señorita*, Rosa will show you to your room," Eduardo said smoothly, nodding at a young woman who seemed to appear out of nowhere. She was pretty, with dark hair and flashing eyes. Her lips were red and pouting, and her maid's uniform did nothing to hide her lush figure.

"Please come with me," she said. "I have a room prepared for you in the guest quarters."

"She'll stay in the same room as me," Sean said, looking down at her proprietarily. "She's mine."

Rosa's mouth tightened, but she nodded and gestured toward the stairs. "Please come with me, *Señorita*."

Sandra didn't want to leave Sean, but he dropped his arm and nodded for her to go. She didn't trust these people, and it occurred to her that she probably shouldn't trust him either. Sean was her enemy, the man originally responsible for kidnapping her, but now she longed for his presence. He seemed so much safer, so much less frightening than all these other people. What was that called? Stockholm syndrome? She'd heard of it before but never dreamt she'd experience it herself.

Something so unnatural shouldn't feel so right—it wasn't fair.

Slowly she followed the maid up the stairs, unconsciously noting the quality of workmanship that had gone into creating the villa. Everything was made of solid wood or tile, all of which bore the signs of hand workmanship. Large paintings hung on the walls, including portraits of strong, menacing-looking Spaniards and delicate white beauties. Family portraits? Valzar's people went back a long way. He must be some kind of aristocrat. Definitely old money.

They came to the top of the stairs and she followed her guide through the gallery. As they left the entrance hall and started down a hallway, she realized the house was even larger than she'd initially thought. The hall was bordered by rooms for a few meters, but as they turned a corner one wall fell away, revealing an open courtyard. Hot air hit her again, but it wasn't as bad as outside. How did they do that?

The house enclosed the entire courtyard, and the whole house seemed to open either onto the gallery above or onto the courtyard itself on the lower levels. There was a large, luxurious swimming pool, as well as immaculately sculpted gardens and several fountains. Even a fake stream had been cleverly designed to run through the grounds, and in the distance she could hear the chirping of birds. It was the most incredible thing she'd ever seen in her life.

Rosa hardly seemed to notice. She abruptly stopped in front of two large wooden doors, then opened them and nodded toward the cool, dark interior. Sandra walked in and the doors closed behind her. She whirled, expecting to see Rosa behind her. Instead, she heard a *snick* sound and realized the maid had locked her in.

"I'LL BE LEAVING IN the morning," Valzar said. He and Sean sat in a tastefully decorated study, a room more likely to be found in a British hunt club than the jungles of the Amazon. "You can reach me any time with Eduardo's help. We have a full communications center here, including subscriptions to all the mainstream news services, as well as more specific researching tools. I've prepared a file of financial information for you. You'll want to know how much money you have, I'm sure, and you'll need to make decisions as to what you'll be doing with yourself."

"Thanks," Sean said, nodding his head in appreciation. He reached out to take the file Valzar handed to him and flipped through it. Right on top was a passport. He opened it up and discovered a worn picture of himself. Next to it was a name, Joe McMurray, Irish national.

"It looks good," he said slowly. "As always, I'm impressed with how thorough you are. You always think of everything, Valzar."

"Thank you," his friend said, smiling briefly. "I've got more for you, though. Here's some information our friends have come up with on your girl. Fresh off the fax."

He handed another file to Sean, and then sat back. Sean took it and flipped it open. The fax transmission was grainy, but there was no mistaking his little toy in the picture. She smiled broadly at the camera. Probably a driver's license photo. He scanned the accompanying information quickly.

Sandra Vicars, 27 years old, single. Residence: 1536 N. Welby, Apt. #6, Danforth, Texas. Five feet, six inches in height, 135 pounds. Next of kin listed as an aunt in New York. Occupation: massage therapist.

He flipped the page, moving on to the next sheet, absorbing the information quickly. Her parents were dead, her only brother in prison for drug trafficking with eighteen years left to go on a federal charge. She had worked at a sports health clinic for five years before starting her own practice, a bad move since the economy had been down for quite a while. Now her bank accounts were all but empty and her practice seemed to be languishing. No criminal history, no suspicions of prostitution.

That caught his eye fast enough.

"It says here she's a massage therapist with no history of prostitution," he said slowly. "She told me she's a working girl. How do you figure that?"

"Keep reading," Valzar said slowly. Sean nodded, eyes quickly covering the page. She was well liked by her neighbors, all of whom were horrified that she'd been taken hostage by a dangerous escaped felon. The press was already hard at work digging up her background for their stories, and the sports clinic where she'd worked was offering a ten-thousand-dollar reward for information leading to her whereabouts. Her former fiancé, a man who had broken up with her two months back, was devastated, and had already made a public appearance on one of the local television stations to beg for her return.

"This isn't good," Sean said, closing his eyes and shaking his head. "I thought she was a pro, someone who would be easy to buy off. That's not going to happen with a woman like this. She'll never understand."

"I know," Valzar said slowly, shaking his head. "I can see you're attached to her, although I can't fathom why. Perhaps it's because you've been without a woman for so long? It doesn't matter, though. You have to get rid of her. I brought in Rosa for you, she can see to all your needs. I'll take care of the Vicars woman."

"No," Sean said, a wave of anger washing over him. The thought of Valzar touching his little toy made his head hurt, and he had to restrain himself from reaching across and hitting the man. "She's mine and I'll be damned if I'll let you touch her. It's not open for discussion."

"Have it your way," Valzar replied, one eyebrow raised and a knowing expression on his face. "She's not a threat to me, it's your ass on the line. Our CIA friends don't like to be embarrassed, and I can assure you that they don't like loose ends."

He handed another sheaf of papers to Sean, then stood and walked over to the full bar that took up the far end of the room.

"Drink?" he asked. Sean nodded his head.

"Scotch," he said, reading the new information restlessly. It was the rough draft of a newspaper article about his escape. Dangerous criminal, riot, hostage, etc. He skipped down toward the end and read about his own death with a sense of grim satisfaction. His hostage had been identified as Sandra Vicars, and her burned body had been discovered with his in the plane wreckage. By the next morning, every one of her friends in Texas would read about it in their newspapers. Somebody would inform the aunt, and Sandra Vicars's small estate would go into probate.

The former fiancé would have to find a new way to get on TV.

Valzar returned with a small glass of amber fluid and handed it to Sean. He drained the drink in one smooth motion, enjoying the way it burned down his throat. Damn, it was good to be out of prison.

"I need to be leaving soon," Valzar said. "Is there anything that you need from me before I go?"

Sean shook his head, lost in thought.

"No, everything you've done for me is wonderful," he said. "I can never thank you enough. I'll let you know when I decide what my next step is."

"Sounds good," Valzar said. He stood, and Sean started to follow him. He waved him off.

"No, sit and relax," he said. "I want you to enjoy yourself for now. It's been far too long since you've had any privacy and space. I'll see you in a few weeks."

With that he turned and left the room, leaving Sean alone with his thoughts.

SANDRA SAT QUIETLY IN the room, unsure what to do with herself. She'd explored a bit, discovering that their bedroom was attached to a large lovely balcony overlooking a private courtyard. There was a spacious bathroom complete with a whirlpool tub and a shower for two.

It was nicer than anything she'd ever seen. What kind of money did it take to maintain a place like this out in the middle of nowhere, and how had it been earned? She shuddered to think. She stood and walked over to the balcony, looking out at the small courtyard. She could climb down easily enough, but there was no point. Even if she managed to get away from the house, she had no doubt the jungle would kill her. She didn't even like camping back home, a jungle trek was completely out of the question as far as she was concerned. She'd last about ten minutes, if that.

No, her salvation lay in convincing Sean to let her go, making him believe she was no threat at all. In all honesty, she wasn't. If she could magically transport herself home right now she wouldn't call the police. Hell, no. She was more afraid of him than anything else, and if he didn't get her, his friend Valzar would.

She had to make peace with him.

The door opened behind her, and she started. It was Rosa, her face cool and hostile.

"I have clothing here for you," she said. "You are probably too fat for it, but it's the best I could do."

She dumped a pile of fabric rudely on the bed and stalked out of the room, slamming the door behind her. Whatever else Rosa might be, she certainly wasn't a potential ally.

She walked over to the clothing and sifted through it, discovering several light, simple cotton blouses and long flowing skirts in bright colors. No bra or underwear, but she could wash out the ones she wore. Not wearing underwear might turn him on . . . anything she could do to keep him interested was a good thing.

She pulled off her oversized male clothing and pulled on the fresh garments. The light cotton blouse had a loose, wide neckline that dipped low. She looked in the mirror, noting that her breasts filled it out nicely, and thankful that they were small enough that she could get away with not wearing a bra. Her nipples formed pert peaks underneath the fabric, and she imagined she could see just a hint of color through the thin cotton. She pulled on the skirt next, enjoying the swirl of it around her ankles. The thin cotton might be enveloping, but she had no doubt direct sunlight would render it nearly transparent. Normally she would have been embarrassed to wear something like this, but now she put her shoulders back and shook out her hair. There was power in being female, a power that she needed to tap into and use to the best of her ability. This clothing was perfect.

She went into the bathroom and had started to rinse out her bra when she heard the door open again. She walked back out and saw Sean standing there. He looked at her with darkened eyes, a thoughtful, calculating expression on his face.

"Hello," she said softly, smiling at him. Things seemed less strange with him in the room. He was her link to reality, the reason she was there.

"Rosa gave me some new clothing," she said unnecessarily. His eyes flickered across her figure, pausing at her breasts, and she thrust them out toward him.

"I like it," she said, walking toward him, allowing her hips to swing as she moved. "It's cool and comfortable."

He stayed silent, so she sashayed closer and rested one hand on his chest.

"You seem tired," she said. "Do you want to come to bed and rest? I'd be happy to give you a massage."

"How about a blow job?" he asked, his eyes boring into hers. "That's more along the lines of what I'd like."

He seemed distant, almost angry, but she nodded her head and gave a hesitant smile. She could do this, nothing to worry about. She reached for the waistband of his pants and unfastened them carefully. He wore boxers, plain white ones. What now? He didn't do anything to help her, and she pulled back hesitantly.

"Where do you want me to do it?" she asked softly. "There's got to be a better place than right here in the middle of the room."

"Why do you care?" he asked, all but snarling. "I thought you were a professional. Don't tell me you're uncomfortable giving me a simple blow job. Drop to your knees and do it."

She nodded, and wished for the thousandth time that she hadn't taken the private appointment with Edgar. Then she gave herself a mental shake. No time for regrets.

Sandra dropped to her knees, grasping the fabric of his pants to steady herself as she swayed. Kneeling, she could see the bulge of his penis beneath the boxers. She took a deep breath, reached both hands up and grasped the waistband. She had done this with Matt, she reminded herself, and at least this guy wasn't lying to her like her fiancé had.

Slowly the boxers came down. His penis bobbed before her, an angry red giant that seemed far too large for her mouth to accommodate. She licked her lips nervously and shot him a quick glance. He still stared at her with that strange angry expression on his face, as if she'd disappointed him. What did he want from her?

It was too scary to imagine what was going through his head, so she turned her attention back to the task at hand. She reached out, tracing the edge of the head with one finger. He didn't respond, although his erection bobbed under her touch. She let her hand fall lower, grasping the smooth, silky shaft with gentle force. Then she leaned her head forward and delicately touched her tongue to the very tip of his length.

He shuddered, and she took it as a sign of encouragement. Sticking her tongue out farther, she swirled it around the head a couple times, allowing her saliva to run out and lubricate his flesh before closing her mouth around the tip. He shuddered, one hand coming to rest on the back of her head and giving an ever so slight pressure as he pulled her closer to him. She opened her mouth farther, allowing his hard length to come into her.

At first it seemed he was so large he would choke her, and she hadn't even gotten more than a few inches past the head. But after a moment her mouth relaxed and opened farther, and he pushed in deeper. She laved her tongue along his length, then pulled back her head and let some of him come free. Time to start the rhythm that drove men crazy. She'd done it for Matt, and he'd always said she was a good little cocksucker, she thought in disgust. Of course, he'd never said anything so foul to her face. He'd waited until they had broken up, and then shared the story of their last time together with all of his friends. Sean might be a kidnapper, but so far he was more of a gentleman than that asshole.

She pushed the horrible thought out of her head, preferring to focus on the task at hand. She found that if she rubbed her hand up and down along his shaft as she sucked at him, he seemed to appreciate it. He still said nothing, but his hand tightened on her hair. She could feel the first drops of his seed in her mouth now, just a little salty taste of what was to come. She had always hated the taste of a man's semen, but his wasn't that bad. Almost sweet in a way, and very pleasant. Without thinking she sucked harder, as if to pull more of the juice from him.

He grunted and she swallowed more of his cock. It had gotten to the point where she actually wanted him in her. She could feel her breasts swelling and knew there was moisture building between her legs. What kind of slut was she? The kind who wants to stay alive, her brain told her firmly. The kind who knows that having sex to survive would be more palatable if she could bring herself to enjoy it. There were worse fates than being forced to make love to a man who was incredibly handsome and more than a little attractive to her. Her situation might be precarious, but she still had a few chances left. She needed to make the most of the fragile bond he'd formed with her.

She sucked him in deeper, wrapping one arm around his waist to support herself. Unconsciously she dug her fingers into the taut muscles of his ass, and he seemed to like the sensation. His cock surged within her mouth and more of his fluid seeped out of his slit.

With every thrust she tried to massage him with her tongue, and each time he pulled out she used suction to hold him as long as she could. Back and forth, in and out. Her hand worked furiously, rubbing along his length and taking care of the parts that her mouth couldn't reach. She felt his other hand grip the back of her head and knew he was getting close.

Then he shifted, letting his legs stand apart a bit, giving her better access. She used the opportunity to reach between his buttocks, allowing her fingers to play with the tightened skin of his scrotum. His balls pulled up close to his body as he neared ejaculation. She suctioned harder, working him as hard as she could, driving him closer to orgasm even as her fingers plucked at his balls, pulling on them lightly.

He gave a startled groan above her and his fingers tightened in her hair to the point of pain. She ignored it, putting everything she had into sucking him. He started to thrust into her harder and she felt the skin of his cock harden almost beyond imagining.

With a harsh cry, he shot his seed into her mouth, all but choking her. The salty, sweet fluid tasted better than any she'd had before, and she found herself swallowing it without feeling sick, as she had so often with Matt. Burst after burst of his essence filled her and she sucked it down greedily.

Finally it stopped. She took a moment to lick around his cock, cleaning it up, and then sat back on her heels. His hands were gone from her head, and when she looked up at him he seemed lost in thought.

"We have to talk," he said after a moment. He wiped his forehead and she noticed a bead of sweat making its way down his temple. "Let's go out on the balcony. It's a lovely place to sit and visit."

Absently wiping her mouth against her sleeve, she accepted the hand he offered. His fingers were hard, filled with strength, and once again she sensed that tension in him. Whatever was bothering him, sex hadn't taken the edge off. When they were sitting comfortably in the two chairs on either side of the small table on their balcony, he turned to look at her.

"I know who you are, Sandra Vicars," he said softly. "And I know you're not a whore, even though you're doing your best to act like one. Now I need to figure out what to do with you. Valzar wants me to kill you, says I need to do it for my own safety. What other options do you have for me?"

SEVEN

*S*HE FROZE, COMPLETELY UNABLE to think of anything to say. How had he figured it out? She could only think of one way.

"Am I really that crappy in the sack?" she asked.

His face froze and he made a sudden choking noise.

"I can't believe you just asked that," he said. "Of all the things you have to worry about right now . . . "

She bit her lip, realizing he was absolutely right. She wasn't thinking at all. She didn't want to think; it was too scary.

"If you just let me go, I promise I won't tell anyone about you," she said. "Honestly, I don't care if they catch you at all. I just want to get out of this alive. Is that so hard for you to believe?"

"I can't let you go," he said slowly.

"You don't trust me, I can understand that," she said, feeling herself grow hysterical. "But I honestly don't know anything about you. I don't even know what country we're in. I don't care, I just want to go home!"

She cut herself off abruptly. She needed to calm down, think clearly. This was her big chance to make a case for herself and she couldn't afford to blow it. She took a deep breath, closed her eyes for a moment and then opened them and peered directly into his.

"Please, let me go," she said softly.

He shook his head slowly, and she thought she saw genuine sadness there. It puzzled her.

"I can't let you go, Sandra," he said slowly. "You're already dead."

She cocked her head at him, and then moaned as his words sank in.

"You're going to kill me right now?" she asked, and something inside snapped. It was too much. She stood abruptly, the chair she'd been sitting in falling to the floor behind her with a loud clanging noise. Fury filled her. It was time to fight back.

"Fuck you," she said in a cold voice. "I hope they catch you and kill you. I hope that they stick you in an electric chair and fry you, and if I had the chance, I'd push that needle plunger down myself."

"They don't use a needle in the electric chair," he said reasonably, standing and reaching out toward her. Sandra stumbled back, desperate to get away from him. She wouldn't go down easy. She balled her fist and slammed it into his stomach with as much force as she could muster. Pain seared through her clenched hand. She shook it, hissing and trying to catch her breath. Apparently unfazed by her attack, he grabbed her upper arms and shook her.

"Settle down and listen to me," he said. She responded by lunging forward and biting into the solid muscle of his chest with every bit of strength she had. Her teeth struck deep and true, and she shook her head like a rabid dog, worrying at his flesh. She brought her knee up to attack his groin, but the motion threw her off balance and he managed to block her attack.

"Stop it," he roared. "Listen to me, I'm not going to hurt you. Please let me explain, and stop biting me."

The words filtered through to her enraged consciousness. Slowly she let up on her attack. Her jaws held him so tightly she had to will them open, the muscles not responding at first. Then she was free, though she noted with some satisfaction that his shirt was rapidly turning red from blood.

Her teeth had hit home.

Good.

Let him feel some of the pain he'd caused her.

"Calm down," he said again. She must have looked like a madwoman, and for a moment, hysterical laughter hovered right on the edge of her throat. She swallowed it back with difficulty. Listening and staying calm was the key to survival.

"What?" she asked after a long pause, her words sounding harsh and forced even to her.

"I'm not going to kill you," he said. "I said you're dead already because according to the newspapers in the United States, your body was found this morning, along with mine. Everyone thinks that we were killed together when our plane crashed. If you go back now, they'll know I'm not dead."

His words sank in slowly, and she shook her head.

"You can't just *do* that," she said. "I don't know what bodies you're talking about, but they'll realize that it's not me. I have dental records. They'll figure it out."

"No, they won't," he said. "The people who would be figuring it out, the investigators, are the ones who planted the evidence. Sandra Vicars is dead, and she'll be buried within a few days. Your family has been notified, as have your neighbors."

She shook her head slowly, willing his words to go away.

"I don't want that to happen," she said slowly. "I was doing something with my life. It isn't fair for you to simply step in and say that I can't go back. You shouldn't be able to take all that away from me."

"It's too late for that," he said softly. "It's already gone. You were in the wrong place at the wrong time, and I'm sorry for what I did. I won't go back, though. I've already been in jail too long for that. I'm done with that forever. I'm dead too, and I'm starting life over as a new man."

"Does that mean you'll be giving back all the lovely money you earned in your old life?" she asked caustically. "Because this place doesn't come cheap, I'm relatively certain of that. If you don't kill me now, when do you plan to do it? After you finished fucking me?"

"That's what I originally planned," he said slowly, his eyes boring into hers with cruel honesty. "Then I decided I'd pay you off. Whores expect that. I figured I'd give you enough money to set yourself up someplace new and we'd both go on our ways. But I somehow doubt that you'll be willing to do that."

She shook her head, thinking.

"Yes, I would," she said suddenly. "If it means I get to live, I'll do it in a heartbeat. Please, let me do it."

"I might let you do that, but I doubt that Valzar would," he said. "He doesn't like to leave loose ends lying about, and you're definitely a loose end. He's already offered to take care of you for me."

"Yes, I kind of picked up on that," she said softly. To her disgust, she could feel moisture welling up in her eyes. She would not cry, not now. She needed to stay strong, to think things through. To convince him that he could trust her. It was her only shot.

"What if I just stay with you for now?" she asked, trying not to sound too coy. "Do we really have to figure all these things out right now? Can't we just have fun?"

He assessed her coolly, nodding his head.

"We can do that."

"Good," she said brightly. "I saw that there was a swimming pool in the other courtyard. Would you like to go swimming?"

"No."

"What do you want to do?"

"Why don't we take a nap?" he asked, raising his hands to cup her head. He wiped at her cheeks with his large, strong thumbs, and she felt moisture there. Damn, she'd cried after all. "You seem worn out."

"I don't think I can sleep," she said honestly. "This has been too much for me—my mind just races trying to figure everything out."

He pulled her against his muscled chest with surprising tenderness.

"You don't have to get everything figured out right now," he said. "You can just relax. Sandra, I promise you, if you do as I say, you won't get hurt. But you're going to have to trust me."

Fat chance, she thought, but she nodded her head against him. He saw her as helpless, as dependent on him for survival. While that might be true, there was no reason for her to give up that easily. As long as she was alive, she could fight.

He released her and reached down with one arm behind her knees. Before she quite understood how he'd done it, she was in his arms, being carried across the room as if she were as light as a feather. He laid her down on the bed very gently and lowered himself beside her. He reached around her with one arm, spooning her and tucking her against his body.

"You don't have to be afraid," he said. "I'm going to take care of you. I'm not quite sure what we'll do just yet, but I'll find a way for you to stay safe. As long as you're with me, nobody will be able to touch you."

His words shouldn't have been as comforting as they were. He was her enemy, her captor. If it weren't for him, she wouldn't be stuck in this situation. But her traitorous body didn't seem to see things that way, and every particle of her being reveled in being held so close. He was big and strong, warm and safe. She felt so comfortable.

He nuzzled the back of her neck through her hair as his hand wormed its way up beneath her clothing to her breast. He cupped her, squeezing slightly, and her nipple hardened. It seemed unfair that it should feel so good. She felt secure with him touching her, happier than was decent under the circumstances.

His hand burrowed through her hair, and his lips became more insistent. She rolled over into his arms and gave herself up in the comfort of the moment. Life was short—she wanted to feel good.

He responded quickly, rolling her beneath him, and for one brief moment they forgot about the future.

EIGHT

*S*EAN STARED AT THE fax, eyes failing to focus.

Why now?

Life had been so perfect. He and Sandra had fallen into a blissful routine. Every morning they'd go swimming, followed by breakfast on the terrace. In the afternoons they'd hike or read, or perhaps even watch a movie. Their dinners were magnificent, celebrations of wine and desire that seemed to go on for hours. Sometimes he'd take her right on the table, other times he'd slowly seduce her over the course of the evening, then whisk her away to their bedroom for nights of wild lovemaking.

It would all come to an end now.

The fax was from Valzar. He needed the safe house for someone else. He didn't give any details, and Sean didn't want to know them. He'd been there for a full month—it was past time for him to start pulling his life together.

It was too easy to relax here, nothing seemed very real to him. That kind of relaxation was dangerous.

The fax made a pointed reference to Sandra too—Valzar offering once more to help Sean with his little liability. Sean leaned back in the chair, closing his eyes and trying to think.

Why had he brought her with him?

He'd told himself at the time that it was because she'd seen him, could identify him to the police. It was a valid concern, but they could have worked around it. More bodies could have been found in that plane crash. The real reason he'd taken her was because he wanted her, he could admit that to himself. He'd seen her, wanted her and decided to take her. He hadn't cared about the consequences. All he'd cared about was getting her under him in bed.

Valzar had lost patience with his little obsession, though. And he was right. They couldn't just stay here in the jungle forever, pretending they were on some kind of bizarre vacation. He could see the questions and the fear in her eyes sometimes, and he knew that it was always in the back of her mind. What would happen to her? Would he grow tired of her? Would he kill her?

Killing her wasn't an option—he'd realized that long ago. He simply wouldn't allow it to happen. She was too special, too beautiful. He wouldn't let anyone hurt her.

At the same time, he didn't know what to do with her. Even if he set her up in a new town with new money, he wasn't entirely sure Valzar wouldn't go after her. His friend was very loyal and very thorough. He'd only held off this long because Sean was actually *with* the woman.

He had to keep her with him. There was no other option. Otherwise, she'd never be safe.

How it would work he couldn't imagine. He had some ideas of what he wanted to do, but he wasn't sure if she'd be interested. Hell, no matter what he did, he'd have to watch her like a hawk. If she got away, her life would be forfeit, and he couldn't allow that to happen.

He'd simply have to find a way to keep her with him all the time. It would be easiest on a boat, he'd decided weeks earlier.

Hell, he'd always liked the idea of living on a boat. There was one waiting for him in the Cayman Islands already, along with his money. Valzar had invested it well, spreading it around the world with a diversity and thoroughness that was frightening. Financially, Sean was doing better than any other time in his life.

He'd always wanted a sailboat, and now he could have his dream. He and Sandra could sail the seas together, exploring exotic ports, swimming in warm waters. All he had to do was convince her to go with him. And watch her every moment of every day when they were in port to make sure she didn't run off.

Of course, none of that changed his central problem—he wasn't entirely sure he could live without her.

That's what scared him the most.

SANDRA LAY OUT BY the pool, idly paging through one of the books she'd found in the library. It was surprising to her how many different English language volumes there were. Of course, the selections were a little out of date. Whoever the reader was, he or she hadn't been here in a while. She suspected there was a story behind that, but she didn't want to ask anyone. Rosa was hostile at the best of times, so light conversation wasn't really an option.

As if summoned by her thoughts, the maid stalked out onto the patio, a grim look on her face.

"You're getting fatter," she said bluntly. "I was doing your laundry, and your shirt is all stretched out."

Sandra rolled to one side and looked up at her.

"It got stretched when Sean pulled it off me," she said sweetly, unwilling to admit how much she enjoyed the disgusted look on Rosa's face.

Rosa glared at her, and then spoke abruptly.

"*Señor* Sean wants to see you inside," she said, a smug look stealing across her face. "*Señor* Valzar needs the house for some-one else and *Señor* Sean has to leave. You know what that means for you?"

Rosa's cold eyes glinted, and she drew one finger across her throat menacingly.

"If I'm lucky, he may even let me do it," she added. With a flip of her hips she turned and left the patio. Sandra felt frozen. She'd put off thinking about this for weeks now.

It had been so easy just to pretend she was on vacation, to sim-ply fall back and relax into the glory that was her time with Sean. And it *was* glorious. She could hardly believe how little she missed her old life. After all, aside from her neighbors and a few friends, she didn't have anyone waiting for her at home. Her brother was in jail, long lost to her even before he'd been sentenced. Her aunt and uncle, the only other close relatives she had left, had never been affectionate to her. They were cold people and had always disapproved of her parents. In fact, she couldn't remember seeing them since the funeral.

It had been easy to put all that out of her mind, along with her bills and her tiny apartment. The only living things that needed her were the houseplants, and she had no doubt that her kindly neighbors had divided those between them. It had been depress-ingly easy for her to drop out of sight. Twenty-seven years old, and nothing of value to show for it.

She shook her head and stood up. That wasn't true. Her life had value. She'd helped hundreds of people at the sports clinic, and had been building a clientele that included many elderly peo-ple who had been soothed by her touch. She had healing hands, and she knew how to use them. She had something of value to offer the world.

She pulled a swim cover-up over the string bikini she wore. It, along with an entire tropical wardrobe, had arrived just days after they'd reached the villa. She had no idea how he'd done it, but Sean had arranged for her to get everything she could possibly need.

She walked slowly toward the house. She needed to talk to Sean, to find out what was really going on. It was too easy to listen to Rosa, and too easy fall into the trap of fear. Yes, her situation was tenuous, but against all rational thought, she found she trusted Sean. He had been good to her, and she knew he got as much pleasure from her company as she did from his. It was time for them to talk.

"THANKS FOR COMING IN," Sean said. She'd found him in the study, his face serious. She'd tied her cover-up around her waist sarong-style. He liked it on her—she knew that from past experience. He'd told her once that nothing was sexier than a woman in a bikini with just a little fabric draped around her hips. She figured it wouldn't hurt to remind him of that when they had their little talk about the future. If ever a time to pull out the big ammo had existed, this was it.

She sat down across from him, deliberately crossing her legs so the fabric fell open. She could feel her nipples coming to attention beneath the thin fabric of her bikini top. The air-conditioning always did that when she first came into the house, and she saw his eyes dart there before returning to her face.

"I got some bad news this morning," he said slowly. She nodded her head.

"Rosa told me."

He grimaced and then shook his head.

"Rosa isn't exactly a reliable source of information," he said.

"No, I try not to pay too much attention to her," Sandra replied. "But it can be kind of hard to feel secure when the only thing I know for sure is that I'm already dead."

"Well, that is a good point," he said dryly. For some bizarre reason she felt a giggle crawling up her throat. She bit it back, knowing it was just tension.

"So, what now?" she asked, laying their central dilemma out on the table.

"I have a plan," he replied. "I've always wanted to live on a boat. A sailboat, to be exact. I've purchased one in the Cayman Islands. I'd like you to join me on it." He sat back, seemingly relaxed. She tried to think, unsure of what response to give. A boat could be good . . .

"I'd like that," she said slowly. "I think we could have a good time on a boat."

It seemed like such an inane statement. Her entire life depended on this man's decisions and all she could think to say was *I think we could have a good time on a boat?*

But she couldn't say what she was *really* thinking. A boat might make it easier to escape. She could even kill him and dump his body overboard. Of course, she didn't have a clue how to sail a boat by herself. But she could watch him. She could learn.

"How big of a boat?" she asked, wondering if she'd have to deal with a crew as well.

"Fifty feet," he said. "Sailboat. We'll have two crew members to start with. They'll be teaching us how to sail it."

"When do we leave?" she asked.

"Tomorrow morning."

"What about documents? Won't I need a passport?"

"That's not a problem," he replied, handing her a manila folder filled with documents. "You have a whole new identity now. Your name is Shannon Bradley, although I think I'll call you Shan. Seems to fit your personality better."

"It sounds like you've got everything figured out," she said slowly. She didn't ask what Valzar thought of the new arrangement, or what he expected would happen to her long-term. It was a good enough sign that he'd gotten her a passport. Sean must plan on keeping her around for a while at least.

"I'll pack my clothes," she said reassuringly, willing him to understand. "I want to make this work, Sean. I'm very highly motivated."

SHE WAS HIGHLY MOTIVATED. He knew that already. In such a short time she had became an important part of his life, yet at heart he knew she was so good to him because she was afraid.

Despite the nice clothing, despite the long nights of making love in the cool air of the villa, Sandra was fucking him to stay alive. Simple, and not particularly pretty. She didn't care about him at all and he couldn't blame her for it in the least.

It was a terrifying thing to realize that your happiness depended on someone else. Especially when it was someone else who had little or no reason to care for you. He'd seen the calculations behind her eyes when she'd asked about the boat. She tried to hide her feelings from him, but she wasn't accustomed to deceiving those around her. She was an innocent, a child compared to him in a thousand little ways. She had no concept of what a man like him could do to another person.

He supposed he should feel guilty, but if he allowed himself to feel guilt over everything he'd done wrong over the years, he'd have killed himself by now. God help him, he would keep her by his side whether she liked it or not. The commitment was made and the plans were already well under way. All he had to do was follow through. She'd be his forever, and if having her was less sweet for her lack of cooperation, then so be it. Having her was worth any price.

NINE

VALZAR WAITED FOR THEM on the dock when they arrived in the Caymans two days later. He was dressed in an immaculate white linen suit, his eyes shielded by dark glasses. With his black hair slicked back and hands tucked in his pockets, he was the picture of a Latin playboy.

Once again, looks were deceiving. He was all business as he shook Sean's . . . no, Joe's hand. She repeated the new name to herself again and again. He was Joe and she was Shannon. That was her new reality and she had to get used to it.

"I see you haven't decided to take care of your little liability yet," he said as soon as they came close. He looked over her coolly, but this time he seemed less hostile. More bemused, and perhaps a bit curious.

"I find that I enjoy her company a great deal," Sean said. "You have no idea what it's like to have a companion who isn't always asking for things."

"That's certainly true," Valzar said, and he gave a rusty laugh that startled her. "My women tend to be fairly high maintenance. Always some new jewel or toy. Speaking of toys, I think you'll enjoy the boat. I had some special modifications made in the interests of meeting your needs."

Together they stepped into the boat, Sean turning to help Sandra. It wasn't large, but still bigger than she'd expected. There was a wide, flat deck broken by a cockpit that thrust up out of it, sort of like a small house. They walked over to the hatch and she stepped in, stumbling at first. Valzar and Sean caught her at the same time, their strong hands pulling at the fabric of her blouse and nearly choking her.

"You need to be careful," Valzar said, his tone low and silky. "It doesn't have steps, it's more of a ladder. You'll do better to go down backwards."

She took a deep breath, steadied herself and slowly climbed down into the darkened interior of the ship's cabin. Her eyes took a moment to adjust, and then she was able to see around her. It was lovely. Everything was done in natural woods and brass.

She was in a small galley, everything tucked away neatly against one wall. A little table curved against another wall. The men joined her, and she shuffled forward uncertainly. It was cramped with all of them in the same small space.

"Go on through the door," Valzar said, nodding to an opening just past the table. She opened the door before her and stepped into another room, this one dominated by a king-sized bed. Small doors flanked either side of the cabin.

"The head is through there," Valzar said, nodding toward one of them. "This will be your room. There's another small one behind the galley, where the crew sleeps. I've stocked it with everything you'll need, and I'm sure you'll be very comfortable."

"What's that other door lead to?" she asked, and then bit her tongue. The last thing she should be doing was opening conversations with Valzar. The man was a snake, and he would swallow her whole given half the chance. She knew it instinctively.

"That's the communications room," he said. "Normally it would be another sleeping cabin, but I've had it converted. You will not be in that room."

"Please don't take that tone with her," Sean said in a cool voice. "You're a good friend, Valzar, but you're overstepping your boundaries here."

Valzar bristled at his tone.

Sandra pressed back against the wall, wishing herself invisible. They were like two large, caged cats, both filled with coiled tension and seeming to take up far more space than was available in the small cabin. The moment passed, and Valzar nodded his head at Sean.

"I see how it is," he said. "You've made your choices. I'll respect them. Just don't forget that I warned you."

"I won't forget," Sean said, his voice equally chilly. "You've done many things for me, but this is something I choose to do for myself."

"I'm sorry," Valzar said. "I'd hoped we could go back into business together, but I can see now that that isn't going to happen. I won't allow her to destroy me too."

"I don't plan on destroying anyone," she said suddenly, and then clapped one hand across her mouth. She'd done it again. Why the hell couldn't she keep her mouth shut? Both men looked at her, startled. "I'm just trying to stay alive and make my way in the world like anyone else. Destroying either of you isn't part of my plan. I have no idea how I'd go about it for one thing. Heck, I don't think I'd want to. At least not in Sean's case."

They looked at her a moment longer, then turned away.

"Wait for us here," Sean said, as if she hadn't spoken. "Valzar and I need to go over the communications equipment."

She nodded her head, feeling as if it were all some surreal dream. They treated her as if she didn't exist in her own right, as if she weren't a human being capable of making her own choices. Neither of them seemed to realize she was more than a doll.

It was extremely frustrating.

The men disappeared behind the door, Valzar having keyed in a series of numbers to the small, electronic lock. She turned, surveying the room once more. This time she noticed more details. There was an inlaid headboard with shelves at the top of the bed, seemingly built right into the structure of the boat. There were several small portholes lining the cabin walls, barely large enough to let in the light, but it would be enough to let the inhabitants tell if it was light or dark.

Behind her, flanking the opposite wall from the bathroom, were drawers and what appeared to be a small closet, all made of the same smooth, highly polished wood that most of the interior featured. She opened one of the drawers and was only slightly surprised to find it already full of women's clothing. She pulled out a lacy black bra and checked the size.

They'd definitely been ordered for her, she noted. Valzar and Sean were nothing if not thorough.

She turned and left the cabin, feeling a bit rebellious. She passed quickly through the galley and then climbed up the ladderlike stairs. On the deck were two large, tough-looking men in suits similar to Valzar's. One of them nodded his head at her, his eyes drifting down her body in an appreciative if distant manner. She didn't bother saying anything to them. They were there to keep her from running away, she understood that. She wondered if they would also be the crew members. It seemed odd, as they were hardly dressed for sailing.

The boat rocked slightly as someone stepped onboard, and she turned to see a small, scrawny man with a scar running across his cheek hopping over to the deck. He carried a black rucksack and wore only a pair of shorts. The two men in suits bristled.

"Don't worry," he said, nodding at them in a friendly manner. "Valzar sent me. I'm one of the new crew members. The other's on his way."

The suits still looked skeptical, as did Sandra. This man hardly looked strong enough to work, let alone run a sailboat as big as this one.

"Oh, I know what I'm doing," he said, giving her a crooked smile and spitting briskly into the water. "I grew up on these islands, lived my entire life on the water. Have my own boat too. Only came out because Valzar begged me to help his good friend *Joe*."

She cocked her head, trying to imagine Valzar begging anyone.

"Call me Skip," he said, moving quickly across the deck and reaching out one hand to her. She took it, and he leaned in close to whisper in her ear. His voice was hardly friendly and harmless now.

"Valzar's told me all about you, chippie," he said in low tones. "I have a great deal of respect for our mutual friend, and don't think for one moment I'd hesitate to slit your throat if I thought he was in trouble."

He leaned back, all smiles again.

"We understand each other?" he asked, his tone friendly once more. She nodded her head quickly, feeling faint. Valzar's presence hung around her like a dark shadow. The man wanted her dead, and she had no doubt that given enough time he'd find a way to make it happen.

Skip nodded to the men in suits and walked quickly over to the hatch. Within seconds he was out of sight, and she stood on the deck, once more looking at the boats around her and wondering if anyone on them could help her.

She thought about screaming, jumping off the ship into the water and making for a friendly face. But none of the boats around appeared to have anyone onboard, and the two men in suits had their eyes glued to her. She wrapped both arms around her body, a part of her wishing they were still at the villa. At least there she'd *known* she was trapped. She'd hated it, but in another way it had been strangely comforting. There had been no hope of escape, and that meant she didn't have to worry about it. All she had to do was lie back, relax and enjoy the bizarre situation in which she'd found herself. It was a place out of time, out of space.

Now she was back in the real world. There were other people around her, places she could run. There were probably even policemen in the harbor, if she could just think of a way to contact them.

Of course, given the way things had gone for her so far, they were on Valzar's payroll too. *Everybody* seemed to work for that man.

THREE HOURS LATER VALZAR was gone, and they were slowly motoring out of the harbor. She sat up on the bow, watching idly as they passed a variety of other vessels, occasionally waving to a friendly face on another boat.

Sean came and sat down beside her. Surprisingly, he wore a

ragged pair of cutoffs and nothing else. He cocked one eye at her startled expression.

"What?"

"I've never seen you look so . . . casual," she said after a moment.

"I don't think I've ever been this relaxed," he replied, leaning his head back against rise of the boat's cabin "Do you realize that we don't have to do anything?"

"Well, we have to leave to sail the boat," she said.

"Yes, but we don't have to do it right now."

"How long will the crew be with us?"

"I haven't decided yet," he said, reaching one arm around her shoulders to pull her close. "Why, do you dislike them already?"

She looked back to where Skip sat at the wheel. Their second crew member, a youngish man named Jose, scampered about, checking ropes and tightening things.

"No, I don't like them," she said. "Did you know that Skip threatened me?"

"I'm not surprised," said Sean, dropping his head to kiss the top of hers. "We already knew how protective Valzar is."

"I think he's jealous of me," she said suddenly. "He wants you to work with him again, and he thinks that I'm the reason you're not. Is that true?"

He stayed silent, rubbing the top of her head with his fingers instead.

"It is true," she said softly. "You can let me go, Sean. I don't want to hurt you. I want you to go on with your life, and I want to do the same."

Once again he didn't reply. Instead, he reached down and tilted her head up toward his. His lips dropped down, kissing her softly on the mouth and then straying across her cheek. His hands started a restless crawl across her body, reaching down and grasping her hips, turning and pulling her until she straddled him. She could feel the length of his erection through her shorts. Liquid fire jetted through her and she melted against him. Why was he able to do this to her so easily?

"Don't," she whispered nervously.

"Why not?" He asked, his tone bemused.

"Because they'll see us," she said, her voice tense, eyes darting across the horizon at the other boats.

"I don't care if they see us," he said softly into her ear. His clever fingers slid her zipper down, even though her hands batted at him, trying to stop him. He took no notice.

"I care," she hissed back. "And I'll bet they care too. Why should they have to put up with that? You're sick."

His hands were inside her shorts now, cupping the curve of her buttocks, rubbing her back and forth against his cock. She shuddered in need, and then took a deep breath before pushing at his shoulders hard to catch his attention.

"I'm not going to do this," she said firmly. "It's simply not going to happen."

He cocked his head at her, then lifted his hands.

"You win," he said.

She sniffed, pulling herself free and sitting beside him on the deck. Her pants were still loose, but she couldn't quite figure out how to fasten them without sitting up on her knees, and that would give the two men behind them too much of a show.

They sat together quietly for a time. The sun had started to lower in the far horizon when he reached over and pulled her into his lap again, this time facing away from him.

She started to fuss, but his hands came up and stilled her.

"Just sit and enjoy the moment," he said softly. His strong

fingers rubbed her shoulders, easing the tension of the moment. She relaxed, and it seemed entirely natural when his hand drifted down her shoulder until it cupped her breast, rubbing absently at her nipple through the soft cotton fabric of her shirt. She leaned back against him, enjoying the sensation. For some reason it didn't seem as threatening as before . . . perhaps because they were out of the harbor. She could feel the bulge of his erection growing beneath her bottom, but he wasn't intent on rubbing it against her this time. He seemed more inclined to simply be close to her, enjoying her presence and the touch of her body.

She felt each breath he took against her back, his muscular chest swelling and falling in time. She let her head loll back against him, enjoying the warmth of the sun as it washed over her with a gentleness that hadn't been present in the jungle.

His hands left her breasts and moved slowly down her body to her stomach to loosen her shirt. His finger slipped under it with deceptive ease, and then started rubbing the soft skin of her belly. It felt so good. She knew she should make him stop, but she couldn't seem to make herself move. Just breathing had become an effort.

Gently, the fingers of one hand slipped beneath her panties. She tried drawing her legs together. Before she got far, his knees came up between hers, and his legs levered hers apart with a gentleness that belied the firmness of his touch. She found herself draped across him, butt in his lap, legs sprawled across his, and she knew in that instant that no matter what he did to her, she wouldn't try to stop him. It simply felt too good.

She shivered when his fingers grazed against her clit. He knew how to touch her, knew how sensitive the little nub was. So sensitive that it was almost painful at times, but his hands were soft. Back and forth, squeezing and working, his fingers slipped across her clit, their way eased by the flood of moisture seeping out of her. When his hand dropped lower, his fingers slid into her opening with a gentleness that was almost embarrassing. So much for her earlier protests. At that moment she didn't care who might see them, all she wanted was to make sure he kept touching her.

Then he pulled his hand away, and she gave a little whimper of protest.

"Wait," he whispered in her ear, and then he wrapped one arm around her waist and lifted her body ever so slightly. His hand dipped down behind her. Then it came back around and he pushed her legs together a bit, pulling her shorts down from behind. When they were around her upper thighs, he brought her back over his lap.

"Just hold still," he said, and she could feel the hot length of his cock against her ass. He lifted her body, and to her surprise, his cock slid neatly into her vagina.

He was big, and he'd always filled her completely, but this time was different. Perhaps it was the strange position, or the fact that her legs were nearly closed, but he seemed to be larger somehow. She could feel every delicious inch of him coming into her, a slow slide from behind that almost made her gasp several times. His hands came around front again, and this time he reached up inside her shirt to work her nipples. She hadn't worn a bra, leaving her breasts completely exposed to his touch. His fingers sought out the stiff little peaks, massaging and pulling on them as he slid into her waiting body with slow determination. She tried to move, tried to wiggle her hips, but he clamped down on her, pinning her to his body with his hands.

"You do what I tell you," he said softly. "I'm in control here."

She nodded her head, a secret thrill running through her. After long seconds of slowly sinking, she reached bottom. She felt his belly against her ass, and unable to control herself, she squeezed him once with her internal muscles. His hips bucked up involuntarily, and he gave a muffled groan.

Not completely in control, she thought wickedly.

Her head still lolled back against his shoulder, arms at her sides and her breasts being worked by his hands. He cocked his hips a bit and then whispered, "Touch me."

She nodded her head, knowing instinctively what he was asking. She flexed herself within and felt an answering twitch from him. One of his hands left her breasts and drifted down, fingers diving between her legs to the tiny nubbin of her clit. As he plucked at it, and then rubbed her firmly, she arched her back and gasped. Inside she clenched him once more, wringing a moan of satisfaction from him.

"That's what I want."

She nodded her head against him and squeezed him again. She supposed she should try and do some kind of steady rhythm, but that seemed impossible. There was a tension within her, spiraling out with every tantalizing rub of his fingers, and she could only respond by clutching him tighter. Every few seconds she forced herself to release, concerned she might be hurting him, but he never said a word. Instead his fingers worked her, rubbing in small circles while pushing with just enough pressure to drive her mad.

Tiny twinges built in her body, and suddenly she was filled with a sense of terrible energy. She couldn't move, couldn't shake it, even though she desperately needed to. She shifted restlessly, clenching and unclenching as his fingers continued their slow, terrible torture of her body.

She was close to the edge. She shivered in tension, and with every breath she clutched at his cock, the solid pressure and presence driving her crazy. She wanted him to move, *needed* him to move. She wanted him to push her forward on the deck and pound into her, crushing her with his weight and filling her with his seed. She wanted that terrible tension to ease, and she'd do anything to make it happen.

She moaned out loud, and he gave a long, low chuckle. His fingers stopped moving, and he whispered in her ear once more.

"What do you want?"

"I want you to fuck me," she said, each word a gasp. "Oh, Sean, I need it so bad. Please."

He laughed, wrapping one arm firmly around her waist and holding her to him as he shifted. As if he'd read her mind, he lowered her face-first before him to the deck. Somehow he managed to pull the shorts off her completely, although she had no clue how. She found herself on her hands and knees on the prow of the boat, speared by his cock and poised on the edge of insanity.

"Do it now," she demanded, her voice hoarse with frustration. His hands gripped her hips, pulled back, and then slammed forward into her with a force that nearly dropped her.

He was huge. He pushed her delicate tissues open, a marauder set on taking her for his own. Eyes closed, it was easy to imagine she was on an old sailing ship, prisoner to a pirate's lust and subject to his every whim. Again and again he pummeled her, each stroke bringing her closer to the edge. His fingers reached around her, dancing cleverly across the center of her desire, and then she exploded into a thousand pieces. She felt her limbs give way, and he lifted her by the waist, her torso dangling forward. He swung her around and laid her facedown across the top of the cabin, arms spread out before her and knees braced on the deck. He started thrusting into her again, and her sensitive flesh cried out for relief. It was too much, she couldn't take any more. Again and again he thrust into her, and she hovered desperately on the brink of another orgasm.

He rode her hard, never giving an inch. Her muscles clenched and unclenched, grasping at him as if she could hold him into her body if she just tried hard enough. Each time he pulled away from her before slamming into her again.

Finally, right on the edge of her orgasm, her head lolled to one side and her eyes drifted open. Standing before her were both of the crewmen, their faces intent. To her horror, Skip rubbed an enormous erection through his pants. Jose stood behind the smaller man, arms wrapped around him, nuzzling his neck. The two men must be lovers.

She wanted to scream at them, to wilt in shame at being seen this way, but all she could do was focus on breathing. She closed her eyes again, pretending they weren't there. Sean thrust into her one more time and she was done.

Starbursts exploded behind her eyes, and every bit of her seemed to cease for one brief, shining moment. She could hear Sean crying out behind her as his seed burst forth into her body. He shuddered against her and then collapsed over her, sucking in deep breaths of air.

Gradually she became aware again of the rocking of the boat, and the soft sighing of the wind as it whispered through the empty rigging. Sean lifted himself and then pulled her back into his lap, cradling her and softly kissing her face. She felt tears building up and welling out of her eyes, and then it washed over her. Everything that had happened, from her kidnapping to this strange new existence hit her at once. She missed her old life, that was true—but what scared her the most was she'd just allowed herself to be fucked by the man who'd captured her, in front of his crew, and all she could think was how much she wanted it to happen again.

What had come over her? What kind of person was she deep down inside?

She sobbed quietly in his arms for what had to be an hour, and he simply held her, rubbing the top of her head and giving her small kisses on her face. Then he led her slowly around the deck to the ladder, and took her down into the cabin. She realized later that she still wasn't wearing her shorts, and that the two other men had seen everything.

It doesn't really matter, though, she told herself that night as she looked in the mirror. *Once two men watch you fuck doggy-style on a boat deck, a little casual nudity isn't all that serious in comparison.*

TEN

*N*O ONE SHOULD BE enjoying life as much as this, she thought in disgust. There was something vaguely obscene about how pleasant it had been over the past week. Much like her time at the villa, she found herself falling into a sensuous routine onboard the boat. The only thing that made it less than perfect was the fact that Skip and Jose were still with them. She and Sean had a much better understanding of how to sail the boat, but Sean still didn't want to get rid of the two men. She wished he would—they frightened her. She knew they still had a lot to learn, but surely there were better people out there to teach them.

They had gone ashore three times, and each time she and Sean stuck together. At first she'd had some dim idea of escape, but it was pretty clear that wouldn't happen any time soon. For one thing, she didn't have any money. For another, she was terrified of Skip. Her earlier fantasies of killing the crew and taking over the boat had been ludicrous. She didn't want to kill anyone, even if she could.

She knew Sean would be able to find her if she ran, but that didn't scare her. He wouldn't hurt her. If Skip found her, though, she'd be finished. He'd gut her without thinking twice, using that long, wickedly sharp knife he kept in his belt. Where the hell had Valzar found a man like that?

Every time he looked at her, he had a smug, smirking look in his eyes. As if he knew all about her and wasn't particularly impressed. She supposed part of it was in her head—after all, it was hard to feel friendly toward a man who'd spied on you during sex. But she wasn't imagining the entire thing. He watched her closely, and his looks weren't friendly. She felt sorry for Jose. Skip wasn't the kind of man she'd wish on anyone, and couldn't help thinking that sharing his bed wasn't the kindest of fates. Still, the young man didn't seem to be unhappy. He did all that Skip asked of him cheerfully, and each night they disappeared to their tiny cabin near the engine compartment without comment.

Despite this, though, things were good. Skip wouldn't be around forever.

She'd made a decision too. She wasn't going to leave Sean. She didn't like everything that he did, but she'd realized something awhile back. She wanted to be with him. Regardless of Stockholm syndrome, she knew her feelings for him were real. She hadn't left anything behind that was so important to her. Living with Sean was good, and she wanted it to continue.

Once she made that decision, things got a little easier.

The days blended into each other, and she spent her mornings lazing on the deck, occasionally dipping in for a swim when they weren't under sail. Much of the time they spent anchored off small islands, many of them almost untouched by the tourist trade. She had always been a strong swimmer, and practicing in the warm Caribbean waters only made her better. So when, on the spur of the moment one evening, he asked her to swim to shore with him, she didn't think twice. She simply pulled off her sarong, revealing the two-piece swimsuit underneath, and dove in.

They played as they swam, him catching up to her and ducking her under, and her pulling him down with her. He was stronger, of course, but in the water he was still vulnerable. They raced the last hundred yards to the beach, wading up out of the water laughing and gasping for air. She ran to a coconut tree beyond the waterline and tagged it.

"I win!" she called, although touching the tree hadn't been part of the original race. In response he growled, running toward her with a look of mock menace. She squealed and ran down the beach. He followed, catching her up in his arms within a few yards and tossing her around as if she weighed nothing.

She clutched his neck, steadying herself, and before long they were both in the sand, laughing and giggling like children.

Sean's face stilled, and he leaned over and kissed her suddenly. It was a quick kiss, hard and full of intent. Humor faded, and he looked down into her eyes, pinning her beneath him with his body.

"I love you," he said suddenly. "I don't know how I was lucky enough to find you, but I love you."

"Thank you," she said softly, not quite ready to say the words back to him. "I wish I'd found you earlier."

"Me too," he said. "Although you'd have had a hard time visiting me. They didn't let anyone in to see me most of the time, let alone women."

She stilled, and a shadow crossed her face. She didn't like being reminded of his past, of who he was. She didn't like thinking of him in Edgar's office and the pool of blood flowing across the floor.

"Will you tell me why you did it?"

"Did what?" he asked.

"Why you had Edgar killed," she said softly.

"Are you sure you want to know?"

For a moment she thought of saying no. It was easier to pretend he hadn't planned a man's death, easier to imagine this was just some wonderful dream free of context and consequences. But it wasn't. If she wanted to be with this man and to truly love him, she needed to understand what he had done.

"I want to know," she said softly. "If you don't tell me, I won't ever understand and maybe there's a part of me that won't trust you."

"What if my explanation makes you trust me less?"

"I don't know," she said softly, trying to be as honest as possible. "I guess we'll take that as it comes. What I do know is that if we aren't honest with each other, we don't have a chance."

He nodded his head slowly, and then rolled off her to lie in the sand next to her. She snuggled into his side as he cradled her with his arm.

"Well, I started out in the Special Forces," he said slowly. "I did that for several years, and then some friends of mine and I decided to go freelance."

"Freelance?" she asked, unsure what he meant.

"We started hiring ourselves out to the highest bidder," he said. "At first we thought we'd be fighting. You know, fearless mercenaries and all that. And we did do some fighting. But what we mostly ended up doing was training other people how to fight."

"I see," she said.

"No, I doubt that you do," he said with a bitter laugh. "But I'll keep telling you anyway. I met Valzar around this time, by the way. He and his family go way back, descended from *Conquistadores*. They've owned and sold people for generations, controlling entire countries. They're always working on some new deal, some new angle. Half the things that happen down here they have a finger in, legitimate and illegitimate."

"He's not a very nice man," she said softly.

"No, he isn't," Sean replied with a harsh laugh. "Although he's a damn good man to have at your back. I hooked up with Valzar because I wanted to get into a new field, hostage rescue, and he had the money. I was tired of teaching peasants how to fight. I knew that whatever I taught them probably wouldn't save their lives, not as long as the guerrillas and the government refused to even consider peace. It's always the peasants who get caught in the middle of these wars. With Valzar's backing, I started contracting with several large insurance companies who offer kidnapping insurance to foreign businessmen."

"I've never heard of insurance like that," she said. "It sounds like a different world."

"That world is all around us," he said softly. "It's just that most people don't have the background to notice it. That's the difference between people like me and people like you. I notice things."

She didn't say anything, knowing he was probably right. She hadn't had a clue something was wrong at Edgar's until she'd walked out of the bathroom. She'd be willing to bet Sean wouldn't have been fooled like that.

"So, Valzar and I started our little business, contracting with these companies and bringing in a nice revenue stream. Most of the time we'd just pocket the profits, and even the occasional hostage situation wasn't too bad. Ninety percent of the time we'd manage to negotiate a ransom for our hostages and get them out safe."

"What about the rest of the time?" she asked.

"We'd go in after them," he said, his voice going lower. "Sometimes it worked, sometimes it didn't. It's a messy business."

She nodded her head, as if she knew what he was talking about.

"So, how did you end up in prison?"

"I ended up in prison because I murdered a man in the United States where I could get caught."

She waited for him to elaborate, but he didn't.

"Why did you kill him?" she asked finally.

"Does it really matter?"

"Yes, it matters," she said.

"I murdered him because he got six of my men killed, not to mention two hostages," he said, his face emotionless. "Their lives were worth twenty-five thousand dollars to him. I learned later that he blew all of it in Vegas the next weekend. That's why I killed him."

She stayed silent for a moment, and then shook her head. "I don't understand," she said softly. "Will you tell me the whole story?"

"Are you sure you want to hear it?"

"Yes," she said softly. "I think if I don't, I'll always question what happened."

"You can't just trust me?" he asked. She looked at him sadly, and then shook her head.

"No, I don't think that I can," she replied. "I wish I could, but you've never given me the chance to make any decisions for myself. If you won't trust me, how can I ever trust you?"

He rolled onto his back and put both hands behind his head. She did the same, looking up at the stars and marveling at how bright they seemed. She'd never seen anything quite like it. If only life wasn't so complicated, she could spend her time with him simply enjoying the life they were leading. But she couldn't just do that, she needed to learn what was really going on, and he was the only one who could tell her. As much as she wanted to turn her brain off, it wasn't happening. She had to know.

"Well, I told you I did contracting with insurance firms," he said. "I was negotiating a hostage release in Sinaloa, up in the mountains. There were two businessmen who'd been snatched off the street in Mazatlán by drug dealers, and I suspect there was more going on between them than a simple ransom demand. Anyway, it was complicated by the fact that one of them had ties to the CIA."

He paused, took a breath, and she drank that in. What a strange world he lived in. Who had ties to the CIA in real life? It sounded like a movie . . .

"When they heard about the situation, they sent an adviser down to work with me. Someone in his office had a big mouth, because they told a coworker, who just happened to be a drinking buddy of Edgar's, about the situation.

"Now, I suppose that any human being with a scrap of decency would have pity on hostages, but not this guy. He decided that information on our operation might be worth something to someone. Edgar found him a buyer. We'd made arrangements for the exchange at a little airfield outside El Quelite. When we arrived the kidnappers were waiting. We were poised to do the exchange, and then they struck."

"Who?" she asked, breathless.

"A rival cartel," he said softly. "Edgar and his pal sold us out to them. They swooped in, killed everyone in sight and took the money. Only five of us got out alive."

She stayed quiet, unsure of how to respond.

"When I recovered from my wounds, I started investigating what happened," he said, his voice growing hard. "I found out about Edgar from one of the drug dealers, and when I came up to the States, I found him and his friend. I watched those bastards for weeks, waiting for just the right moment. I waited until they went out drinking one night and ambushed them in the parking lot. I killed the CIA leak first, but I underestimated Edgar—he pulled a gun on me and shot me. I woke up handcuffed to a hospital bed."

"What did he tell the police?" she asked softly.

"He said he thought it was a random act of violence, that I'd been trying to mug them," Sean said softly. "I didn't bother contradicting him. I figured that I'd do better pretending it was a crime of opportunity rather than a hit. They're a little too excited about the death penalty in Texas to take chances. They offered me a plea bargain and I took it."

"And Edgar just got away with it?" she asked softly.

"Until I got back to him," Sean said with dark satisfaction. "He killed my men, Sandra. He deserved to die."

"Why did you get caught in the first place?" she asked. "I've seen you in action. I wouldn't have thought a man like Edgar could get the drop on you."

"Honestly?" he said, his voice still toneless. "I lost my cool. I'd intended to follow them for a while, learn their habits and make it a clean hit. Instead I lost my temper. When I saw them drinking and laughing together I couldn't stand it. I had to get them. And I had to do it right then."

"I guess I can understand that," she said softly. "The world probably is better off without him. Did you ever consider going to the police with the entire story? I mean, before you decided to kill them yourself."

He gave a quick bark of laughter.

"No, that was never an option," he said. "Not with the CIA involved. They don't like any kind of publicity, and they'll do whatever it takes to keep information on their little mistakes from coming out. They preferred to let me handle things, and when I finally found a way out of prison, they were more than happy to assist in my disappearance. They owed me, you see."

"Yes, I can see that," she said. She rolled over toward him and ran one finger along the bridge of his nose. In the moonlight he was little more than a stark profile beside her, cool and almost untouchable.

She let her finger trail down the smooth curve of his throat, then trace along his chest until she reached his stomach. She laid her hand flat, watching his chest rise and fall, and wondered how she had ever met up with this strange and terrifying man. She knew then, right there in the moonlight, that he was worthy of her love. She was glad Edgar was dead. He'd deserved what Sean had done, no questions asked. She just wished he'd been able to get to him sooner, that he hadn't wasted five years of his life in jail.

"I love you," she said suddenly, realizing it was true. He froze, a profound stillness coming over him. Even his breathing seemed to stop, and then his hand came up over hers and clenched it tight.

He started to reply but was cut off abruptly as a booming explosion tore through the night.

He rolled over her suddenly, one hand covering her mouth. He pushed her head down into the sand, his body covering and protecting hers. A second explosion ripped through the darkness, and then silence drifted back over them.

"I'm going to let you look up," he whispered in her ear. "Don't say anything and don't get up, or they might find us."

She nodded her head, and he shifted his weight. She rolled over and looked out across the water. A mass of fire lit up the night where their boat had been moored.

"Skip and Jose were on there," she whispered numbly. "We have to get help!"

"They're dead," Sean said softly. "There's no way they could have survived that. We're supposed to be dead too."

She looked at him blankly.

"Why else would someone blow up the boat?" he asked. "They wanted to kill us, Sandra. The good news is that they probably think they succeeded. We just have to keep it that way."

ELEVEN

*S*ANDRA TRUDGED THROUGH THE underbrush doggedly, ignoring the insects buzzing around her painfully exposed flesh.

She felt like a boiled lobster.

The hot sun tore into her pale skin ruthlessly, and she cursed the skimpy bikini she'd worn for their midnight swim. Still, she struggled forward, refusing to complain. Whining wouldn't do either of them any good.

The night had seemed endless. Sean had insisted that they remain still and out of sight until morning, and even then they'd spent a few more hours hiding. He'd gone out looking around a few times and had spotted two men watching the remains of the boat. They'd left a few hours later, climbing into a jeep and driving off down the sandy beach.

She'd thought they should stay and wait for help. After all, there couldn't be that many midnight explosions on the island. Someone was sure to notice eventually. Sean nixed that idea immediately, telling her it was too dangerous. Whoever rescued them would probably talk about it to someone else, and then the attackers would learn they were still alive.

So here they were, trudging through the jungle in the direction Sean insisted would lead them to a village. She had no idea what they would do when they arrived. After all, it couldn't be too often that white tourists in bathing suits appeared out of the jungle asking for a phone, but he seemed to know what he was doing. She certainly had no clue, so she was content to let him lead her.

Surprisingly, they reached the village after only an hour of walking.

She'd expected them to go right in, but he'd installed her in the bushes and went by himself. Ten minutes later he was back wearing a loose pair of cotton pants held up with a rope and a faded, button-up shirt. When he handed her a ratty T-shirt and oversized jeans, she'd never been so happy to see anything in her life.

"Where did you get these?" she asked.

"I traded my watch for them," he said. "The farmer said he'd give us a ride into a town with a phone too."

"Won't he tell people about us?" she asked.

"Probably," he said. "Although I've asked him not to. The people in this village are very closemouthed, and they don't like outsiders."

"How do you know that?"

"I research every place we go," Sean replied. "It isn't an accident that we came to this particular island. You never know when you might need a bolt-hole, and a small village like this one can be a great place to lose yourself. I promised him more money if he gets us out of here without anyone seeing us."

She nodded her head, amazed at how he managed to pull these things off. He handed her a small pair of sandals made from braided rope and she slid them on her feet. He reached down, pulled her up, and they were off. Twenty minutes later they crouched beside a narrow, one-lane track. After what seemed like hours, they heard the sound of a sputtering engine. Sean stood up and waved as he recognized the farmer, who drove a pickup that had to be at least thirty years old. The cab was tiny, but she felt so happy to be on her way to civilization that she didn't mind sitting awkwardly on Sean's lap.

Two hours later, after bumping across the road and hitting her head on the roof of the truck every two or three minutes, she had a blinding headache. She hardly even noticed when they pulled out of the jungle into a small village. She did notice, however, when the truck passed through the village and hit a paved road. Their surroundings grew steadily more modern until they reached what could only be a tourist area, several hundred feet of beachfront lined with graciously aging hotels. Twenty years earlier this place had been a real hot spot.

The truck pulled to a halt in front of one of the buildings. With Sean's muttered thanks to their driver in a language she didn't understand, and they were left standing in front of the hotel as two startled doormen looked around for their bags.

Sean had her sit in the lobby, and half an hour later he came back and escorted her up to a well-appointed suite, possibly the best the hotel had to offer. She collapsed on the bed, utterly exhausted, and barely paid attention as he went into the other room to talk on the phone. After awhile he joined her, pulling her into his arms and kissing the back of her neck softly as they fell asleep.

THE NEXT MORNING SHE found herself alone. She considering calling down to the desk and asking for him, but she didn't want to do anything to draw attention to herself. After all, someone had tried to kill them. The last thing she needed was to call down and ask for him by name, especially if he hadn't used his real name. She didn't even know what names they were using. Was he Sean or Joe?

Instead she took a long hot bath and tried to calm her thoughts. She seemed to be getting used to this life on the run, she realized wryly. The things that would have driven her crazy just a few months ago, the uncertainty, the fear, she managed to push to the back of her mind. For the first time in her life she was living for the day, not the future. Refreshing in a way. Zen.

She snickered at the thought as she toweled off and pulled on a fluffy bathrobe. She walked into the main room. There was a shadow, a man talking on the phone. Her heart leapt. Sean? No, Valzar.

"What are you doing here?" she asked coldly.

He dropped the receiver back in the cradle, and then turned to her.

"I'm here to take you away," he said, eyes watching her without expression.

"What do you mean?" she asked. "Sean won't like this and you know it."

"I'm here because Sean asked me to come," he said softly. If she hadn't known better, she might have said he had pity written on his face.

"That's not true," she replied. "Sean doesn't trust you. He wouldn't leave me alone with you."

"Yes, I'm afraid it is," he said. He walked toward her, and she clutched the robe more tightly to her chest, backing away from him. He smiled, but there was no happiness in his expression.

"For reasons I still don't understand, he cares for you," Valzar said. "He's worried. Last night scared him, made him realize that his enemies are still out there. He needs to be alone, *chica*. You're his weakness."

She shook her head, denying it.

"I'm not his weakness, you are," she said bitterly. "You're the one who got him into this, and for all I know you're the one trying to kill him. You need to leave us alone."

"You need to realize what kind of man you've been sleeping with," Valzar said. "Sean is not the kind of man who can settle down, who can afford a family. None of us are. Sean needs to be free so he can do his work."

"Sean's tired of his work," she said, her voice cold. "He's been out of your business for five years—all he wants is to sit back and enjoy his freedom. Why can't you just let him do that?"

"I'm not the one he has to protect," Valzar said, his voice gentle. "You are. He sent me here because he wants me to spirit you away, to make you disappear. He wants you to be safe. You've made him desperate, and desperate men do foolish things."

"You've made no secret of the fact that you want me dead," she said. "Why should I trust you now? This is some kind of game you're playing, and I won't be your pawn in it."

"There's a spy in my organization," Valzar said softly. "It's the only way they could have found the two of you. That means they knew I wanted you dead. I'm the perfect person to make you disappear. That's why Sean asked me to help, because it's my fault. I owe him more than I can repay."

"You're full of shit."

He stepped closer to her, invading her space. He smelled warm and male, and for an instant she could imagine that some women would find him very attractive. Fools who weren't smart enough to realize the man didn't have a soul.

"I'm not full of anything but the desire to help my friend," he said, touching her shoulder. She stiffened. "He has asked me to help you, and I'm going to do that, regardless of what I think should be done with you. I've given him my oath."

"You can't force me to do anything," she said.

"Yes, I can," he said. "You can come easily, or I can have my men inject you with a sedative and take you out while you're unconscious. I don't care either way."

They glared at each other for a long, tense moment, and then she let her gaze fall. She wasn't going to win this way.

"All right," she said quietly, disgusted by the submission she could hear in her voice. "Let me get dressed."

TWELVE

IVE STORIES WAS A long way to fall. Just looking over the edge of the balcony made her dizzy, but she thought she had several minutes before Valzar came into the bedroom to check on her. She'd be damned if she'd go with him quietly. Somewhere out there Sean was fighting for his life, and she wasn't going to leave him to do it alone. Fuck Valzar.

Taking a deep, calming breath, she swung her leg over the railing and set it firmly on the ledge. She figured she had no more than seven minutes at the most before he became suspicious. Clutching the side of the building, she slid one foot forward and then followed it with the other until she reached the next balcony. She climbed over the rail with relief and tried the door. Locked, naturally. Taking another deep breath she crossed the balcony and stepped back out onto the ledge. There weren't any more balconies on this side of the hotel, but she wasn't far from the corner and she hoped that there was something around it.

Luck was with her.

When she reached the corner and peeked around, she could see the roof of the building next door. There was a narrow gap separating the two hotels, and not far below she could see a metal fire escape. If she could get around the corner, she'd be able to jump onto the fire escape and climb down.

Easier said than done.

The gap between the buildings wasn't that wide, but the roof was a good six feet below her. She had never been particularly athletic. Visions of broken limbs danced through her head, but then she reminded herself what was at stake.

Her future with Sean.

Damn, she was tired of other people making decisions for her. If staying with Sean meant risking her life, that was her decision to make. He had no right to send her away with Valzar, none at all. She needed to get out and find him and explain that little fact to him.

She'd finally had enough.

Taking a deep breath, she whispered a prayer and launched herself across toward the other roof. She hit with a thump, rolling several times before coming to a stop. There were scrapes on her hands and she was sure she'd be sore after awhile, but none of that mattered. She'd done it.

Sandra pulled herself up, all too aware of how visible she must be. She crawled over to the edge of the roof, looking for the fire escape. For the first time she wondered why the other hotel didn't have one. The thought was rather chilling. If there had been a fire, she'd have been out of luck. . . . Even more chilling was the state of the fire escape she needed to use now. It was rusty and seemed to sag away from the building in several places. She reached out and pushed on it gingerly and it made a creaking noise.

Good Lord.

She reminded herself once more why she was doing this. She was tired of being passive, tired of other people telling her what to do. This time it was going to be about *her*, and *her* needs. She needed to be with Sean, and she'd be damned if she was going to let him get away. Screw everyone else.

She reached one leg over the side and tested the fire escape. It seemed to hold the weight she put on it. She lowered herself gingerly off the roof and onto the rickety contraption. It made a creaking, moaning noise, but nothing else happened.

I can do this, she told herself.

Down she went, trying not to imagine what it would feel like to plunge four stories. She didn't think about whether anyone could see her, about whether Valzar had goons posted all around the buildings. All she could think about was climbing. One foot down, then another. Step after step, rung after rung, until she was on solid ground. She looked around and realized that nobody watched her. She'd done it. She was free.

She found her way along the side of the building until she reached the alley running behind it. She moved down the alley as quickly as she could, wondering what to do next. She had no idea. For all she knew Sean wasn't even on the island any longer. How was she going to find him, and how would she convince him to allow her to stay with him? She had no money, no papers. Officially she didn't exist.

She walked down the narrow streets, wishing desperately that she'd paid better attention when they'd arrived. A small group of mixed-race children started tagging along after her. She ignored them at first, but it got harder after awhile. They swarmed around her, eyes filled with curiosity and mischief. What did they want?

"Yo, lady," one of the kids said, and she whirled. An English speaker!

"You wanna take my picture, lady?" the girl asked. She looked to be about ten years old, and her eyes gleamed with capitalistic fervor. "You give me dollah, lady, I let you take picture."

"I don't have a dollar," she said quickly. The girl rolled her eyes and spoke quickly to the children around her in rapid Spanish patois.

"You lost, lady?" the girl asked after a moment.

"Yes," she admitted. "Can you help me?"

The girl cocked her head, and another child spoke to her again. She nodded at him, and the other kids clapped their hands.

"We gonna help you, lady," the girl said. "You look pretty sad all alone here. You gotta tell the people at the embassy that we're good kids, though, that we help you."

"There's an embassy here?" she asked, suddenly filled with relief. She could get help!

"Little one," the girl said. "You got papers?"

Sandra shook her head. The child shrugged, and then started walking.

"You come with me," she called over her shoulder. The children seemed to think she needed their escort, because most of them started walking with her as she followed the girl. People watched as the strange little convoy moved down the street, and she wondered if it was foolish to allow such a spectacle to be made of her "escape." But it wasn't really as if she had much choice, she reminded herself. She had no idea where she was going or what she was doing. Hopefully they could give her some direction at the embassy. At the very least, they should be able to tell her where she was and give her access to a phone. She could call Valzar and demand that he have Sean call her, she thought suddenly. If she called from the safety of the embassy, there wasn't anything he could do to her. She could threaten to tell them everything if he didn't put her in touch with Sean immediately.

She smiled, feeling rather pleased with herself. She had it all figured out.

After walking for twenty minutes the streets were getting noticeably cleaner, and then she saw an American flag in the distance. Her heart lifted, and she felt a burst of patriotic pride that she'd never felt before. How beautiful it was in the distance! In that building there were people who could help her—she would be completely safe with them. It was a wonderful feeling.

A few blocks from the lovely gated complex the little girl turned into another alleyway.

"The embassy is over that way," Sandra said, confused.

"You gotta go this way to get to gate," the child replied. "Much faster."

Sandra shook her head, but the girl had helped her so far. Within seconds they turned again and she found herself in an open courtyard. The children started giggling, and she realized something was very wrong.

She spun around, ready to go back toward the flag, but two large, armed men were already there, blocking her escape. Valzar strolled out of the shadows, shaking his finger at her disapprovingly.

"Now, Sandra, that's no way to behave," he said. "If you keep this up, I'll start to think you don't like being around me. Wouldn't that be a shame?"

THIRTEEN

*W*RETCHED CHILDREN, SHE THOUGHT darkly. How could she have trusted them? Their little eyes glowed as Valzar pulled a handful of bills out of his pocket. He'd given one to each child, patting them on the head as he did so, and spoke softly in their own language. She might have been impressed with his thoroughness if she wasn't so disgusted. Bastard.

He'd used her—she'd gone through all that stress for nothing. She was no better off than she'd been before.

"You do realize that I could tell Sean you died trying to escape," he said as he escorted her out of the alley into a waiting SUV. A driver and one of Valzar's thugs sat in the front. "Sean would never know the difference."

"Why would he care?" she asked softly.

"You're a fool if you don't know the answer to that question," Valzar said. "He's waiting for you to leave, Sandra. He wants you to be safe and he trusts me to make sure it happens. I've never known him to hold back his plans for anyone. He cares about you a great deal."

She sat passively beside him in the backseat as the car started moving.

"Do you ever do your own dirty work?" she asked bitterly, nodding her head at the man in the front seat. Valzar smiled briefly, his teeth gleaming in the darkness of the car. The tinted windows screened them completely from whoever might be waiting outside.

"Yes, I do my own dirty work," he said. "You'd probably be surprised at how much time and effort I put into running my little business empire. But that's not really something you need any further information on at this point."

She nodded her head, wishing she could kick him. She watched as they drove past the lines of buildings. Before long there were more and more patches of green. Then they were turning off the paved road, entering the jungle she'd come to despise.

"Where are we going?" she asked.

"To a small airstrip," he replied. "Sean and I would prefer it if you didn't have to answer any awkward questions at the airport. This way you won't have to."

"How far do we have to go?"

"It will take at least an hour," he said. "Perhaps two. You might wish to try sleeping."

She nodded, doubting sleep was possible. Her heart pounded from the attempted escape. Smug bastard.

Valzar shrugged his shoulders, and she glanced quickly at the door. Locked, naturally. She waited until she was sure nobody watched and tried to push back the little button. Nothing. Clearly, they'd disabled the locks. Perhaps there was some other way to escape. She pretended to go to sleep, slowly counting to a thousand. By the time she was done, the men around her seemed fully relaxed and settled into the drive. The bodyguard talked to the driver quietly, occasionally leaning forward to fiddle with the radio. She could see his gun, nestled between the seat and door in front of her. It wasn't a big gun, but she figured it would do the trick if she could get her hands on it.

Still pretending to be asleep, she slowly slumped forward. Moving very carefully, counting to a hundred between each little shift, she edged her hand forward and waited for her opportunity. The road was bumpy, barely a track through the brush at this point. When they hit the next big pothole, she lunged her hand forward and grabbed the gun. She jerked it back and slid it under her leg, then squawked in pain.

"I hit my head," she said shrilly, and the men jumped. "This is insane. I need to go to the bathroom. You need to stop the car right now."

The driver looked in his mirror to Valzar, who nodded his head with a vaguely disgusted look.

"Go ahead," he said. "Stop the car."

They stopped right in the middle of the dirt road, and then the driver unlocked the door with a click.

"Get out and go," Valzar said. He nodded at the men and said something in Spanish. The driver opened his door and stepped out. He strolled around to the front of the car, pulling out a package of cigarettes. The bodyguard joined him, while Valzar stepped out and stretched.

She slid out her own door with a whine, went behind the SUV, unfastened her jeans and crouched as if to relieve herself. She took a moment to study the gun until she was sure how it worked. It was simple enough, exactly like she'd seen hundreds of times on TV and in movies. She went over it once more, checking to make sure the safety was off, and then rose, ready to make her move.

She came up behind Valzar and raised the gun steadily.

"Be still and do what I say," she said quietly, her voice as cold as she could make it. She wanted him to *know* she'd shoot. He turned to her, a look of slight surprise on his face, followed by a slow smile.

"Well this is a surprise. I wonder if Sean has any idea how violent his little toy can be?"

"Be quiet," she snapped. "I'm not interested in listening to your bullshit. Have the driver toss you the keys, and then have them both walk away from the car."

"And if I don't?" he asked.

"I'll kill you and take your bodyguard hostage," she said. "I don't like you, and I'm not going to let you send me away from Sean. I'm feeling more than a little pissed at you right now. Don't test me, because you'll end up dead."

He studied her for a moment longer, and she let some of the hate she felt toward him show in her eyes. He'd offered to kill her more than once, threatened her continually. She'd do what had to be done.

He must have believed her, because within moments he held the SUV keys and the men were walking back toward town.

"Do you have a cell phone?" she asked. He nodded his head.

"I want you to get on the line and call Sean. I want you to tell him that he needs to meet us at the airfield."

"How do you know I can reach him?" he asked.

"You'd better hope you can," she replied. "I'm going to get tired eventually, and when that happens, I'll have to shoot you and make a run for it. If I let you go now, you'll kill me, and believe me when I say that if I have to choose between my life and yours, you'll lose."

He nodded his head again, and reached into a pocket. She watched closely, half expecting him to come out with another weapon. What she'd do if he did, she didn't know. She wouldn't back down, though. It was too late for that.

His hand came out again with a small flip phone, and he flicked it open with a nonchalance that belied their situation.

"Sean, your woman has taken me hostage," he said after a moment, speaking as casually as if describing an insect he'd found on his shoe. "She's going to kill me if you don't meet us at the airstrip."

He looked at her and held the phone out.

"He wants to talk to you," he said.

"Nope," she answered, shaking her head. "I'll give him two hours to get out there. If he doesn't come, I'll shoot you in the knee. It will get worse after that."

He nodded slowly and relayed the message to Sean. Then he closed the phone with a smooth click and nodded toward their vehicle.

"Shall we?" he asked, his voice almost gallant.

"After you," she replied mockingly. He gave her a slight bow and opened the door for her.

AN HOUR AND FORTY-FIVE minutes later she was starting to sweat.

If Sean didn't show up soon, she would have to shoot Valzar. She didn't want to do it, couldn't imagine inflicting that kind of damage on another human being. What did a man's knee look like after a bullet tore through it? She was desperately afraid she'd find out in the next fifteen minutes.

Holding him hostage was tiring. She knew he had men all around her, knew that they probably had guns. Every moment she expected to feel a sniper's bullet hit her, but so far they were doing well. They were holed up in the tiny concrete block hut on the edge of the airstrip, and she felt relatively safe. It would be hard for anyone to get a clean shot at her, at least while she was inside. Of course, she'd had the element of surprise on her side when she'd brought him here. Leaving the shack would be much trickier, if not impossible.

Seven long minutes passed, and for the first time she began to seriously doubt that Sean would come. Valzar watched her, eyes following every nervous tick of her feet, monitoring the trembling of her hands with a calm that was creepy. Then his cell phone rang, the sudden noise making her jump. She nodded at him to answer it, and he did.

"It's Sean," he said softly. "He's waiting outside."

"Tell him to come in," she said. "No weapons, please."

He gave Sean the message, and she stood, directing him to join her with a wave of her gun. A moment later there was a knock on the door.

"You can come in," she called. Sean stepped inside, looking at her with a strange expression on his face.

"This is a little extreme," he said, gesturing toward her hostage.

"Oh really?" she asked caustically. "It seems pretty in line with everything that's been happening around me lately. One more hostage situation isn't much, all things considered."

"What are you hoping to accomplish with this?"

"I've made a decision," she said softly. She looked to Valzar, and then nodded her head toward the door. "You can go, asshole."

Valzar's expression didn't change. He strolled out of the building without a second glance at her, although he shared a meaningful stare with Sean. What that meant she had no idea, and she didn't care. They would be leaving soon anyway. Sean started toward her, and she waved the gun at him threateningly. He froze.

"Like I said," she continued. "I've made a decision. I'm tired of you calling the shots in this relationship. I'm an adult and I can think for myself. We're staying together whether you like it or not."

"You do realize how ridiculous this is?" he asked softly. "You can't take me hostage and force me to be in a relationship with you."

"Oh really?" she asked quietly, cocking her head at him. "Funny, because that seems to be exactly what you did with me."

They both fell silent for a moment as he considered her words. Then he took a step toward her and reached for the gun. She shook it at him warningly, and he laughed.

"You aren't going to shoot me," he said. "I already know that. You just told me you want to be in a relationship with me."

"Correction, I *am* in a relationship with you," she said. "Remember? We've been living together for almost two months now. I don't even have a home to go back to. You kidnapped me, made all the decisions for me and then decided to get rid of me when things got tough. I hate to break it to you, but things don't work that way in my world. We're in this together, and don't you think for one minute you'll make it outta here without me. You won't."

"Why are you doing this?" he asked, his expression genuinely puzzled. "Valzar wasn't going to hurt you. Even after you took him hostage he wouldn't have hurt you. You belong to me, and he would never take anything of mine away without my permission, no matter what he says."

"Listen to yourself!" she replied, disgusted. "That's what you don't get! I don't *belong to you*. I'm a free human being, and I make my own decisions. You're going to take me with you and we're going to build a life for ourselves. We've come too far for you to try and weasel out of it."

He seemed stunned for a moment, and then he shook his head.

"You silly fool," he said. "Don't you understand that I'm trying to protect you? There are people who want me dead. They blew up my boat! If you stay with me, they'll kill you too."

"They think you're already dead," she said, rolling her eyes at him. "And even if they don't, we'll fight them together. I'm not some kind of doll who can't talk and think and act, you know. I have this gun and I'm willing to use it to protect what we have. Don't imagine for one moment I wouldn't. What kind of pansy do you think I am?"

He looked at her steadily for a moment, and then shook his head.

"I'm not going to change your mind, am I?"

"No," she said, shaking her head firmly. "You aren't. You can do this the easy way or the hard way, but it's going to end the same."

"Do you have any idea how much seeing you hold that gun is turning me on?"

His comment was so startling that she blinked, unsure of what to say. In that instant he struck, pulling the gun away from her and flinging it across the room. He twisted her arm up behind her, pulling her against his body. She'd gone from being completely in charge of the situation to a helpless hostage in less than ten seconds. She felt the length of his body up and down her front, the unmistakable bulge of his erect cock pushing against her belly.

She looked up at him, tears welling up in her eyes as she realized she'd failed. He'd just been toying with her. She'd been easy prey for him, and all her thoughts of empowerment meant nothing.

She wanted to bash herself over the head in sheer disgust.

His eyes searched her face, the warmth she'd seen in them earlier completely gone. Instead there was a need, a desire so intense she could hardly fathom it. His mouth came down over hers, and his strong hands crushed her against his body.

Unable to stop herself, she followed his lead, pushing her body against him. She wanted to crawl into him, drink up his essence. The layers of clothing between them scratched at her and she wanted them gone. She needed his touch *now*.

He felt the same. She could see it in his every move, feel it in the urgency of his hands against her body. He wasn't holding her arms prisoner any longer. She was free to hold him, and she wrapped them around his neck as he hoisted her in his arms. He carried her over to the low, metal desk, lips glued to hers. His tongue thrust in and out, giving her no chance to reciprocate. He wanted her and he was taking her. It was that simple.

Then he pulled his mouth away from hers. Of one mind, they scrabbled at their clothing. Her jeans came off and his came down, and then they were in each other's arms once more. He lifted her bottom onto the desk and pulled it forward to the edge. His cock thrust into her. Hard.

His entry was harsh, no room for tenderness in his touch. He was taking her, claiming her, just as he'd claimed her initially. Again and again he thrust into her, and she pushed back, more aroused than she'd ever been in her life. If he was a stallion mount-ing her, she was the mare. She wanted him, needed him. When her orgasm hit, she clawed at him, gasping and bucking like a wild animal. Then he burst within her, shooting his seed high into her body. They collapsed together, spent, their heaving breath echo-ing through the small concrete hut.

"Wow," she said softly, unsure of what should happen next.

He gave a little laugh and leaned his forehead against hers, eyes closed for a moment. Then he opened them and looked directly into her face.

"What now?" he asked.

"I won't let you leave me again," she firmly. "I'll hunt you, Sean. You don't have the right to end this without me. We're together now, and there's no way you can deny that."

"You're right," he said softly. "We are together now, and I don't have the right to end it by myself."

She pulled back, startled by his easy capitulation.

"How long do you think I would have lasted without you?" he asked, laughing lightly. "By the time I got the phone call from Valzar, I was about to call him. I couldn't do it, I couldn't live without you. I know it's dangerous for you to stay with me, but I'm not going to give you up."

"I'm not going to give you up either," she replied. "We'll just take things as they come. We've been pretty lucky so far, you know."

"Lucky?" he asked, snorting. "How do you figure?"

"Well, neither of us has killed the other yet," she said lightly. "Considering the circumstances, I'd say that's pretty damn lucky. So now what?"

"Well, we have a plane waiting for us," he said. "Valzar has a leak in his organization, so he's not setting anything up for us this time. We're hoping that whoever blew up the boat doesn't realize we're alive. They're going to report that four bodies were found instead of two. If they believe the reports, we may be safe."

"I don't want to endanger anyone else," she said seriously. "You know, it's one thing for you and me to make a decision like this. Skip and Jose didn't know what they were in for."

"Yes, they did," Sean said quietly. "There weren't any secrets there. But I agree with you, I don't want to see that happen again. From now on it's just you and me."

"So, I guess we go out now?" she asked, looking toward the

door. "I would imagine some of the people out there are pretty pissed off at me right now. I hope you'll stand between us . . . "

He laughed and dropped a kiss to her nose.

"Don't worry," he said quietly. "I'll always be with you, whatever comes next. We're in this together. Although I do have one concern."

"What?" she asked, suddenly anxious.

"I think we should put our clothes back on first."

Valzar leaned back against the jeep casually, hands in his pockets. Sean and his woman were taxiing down the small, primitive runway in a little Cessna. Soon they'd be gone, and he had no idea if he'd ever hear from them again. It would probably be for the best if he didn't.

There were serious flaws in his organization, leaks that needed to be plugged, sources that needed to be cut off. Two good men had died in that boat blast, and it was just dumb luck that Sean and Sandra were still alive.

He suspected that Rosa might have something to do with it, although he wasn't sure. He had a lot of suspicions. Now he just had to give his people enough rope to hang themselves. Then the entire house of cards would fall, and he could pick up the pieces of his organization and move forward.

The Cessna was in position now, and he could hear its engines roaring as Sean started his takeoff. The little plane charged down the runway, and then the wheels lifted off the ground. Up into the air it soared, smoothly sailing over the treetops until it was a speck in the distance. Then it was completely gone.

Something like sadness washed over him. Sean had been a good friend for many years, and he was sorry to see him go. He didn't like to admit it, but he felt something else too. Envy. Envy touched with jealousy. Sandra was a woman willing to fight to the death for her man. When he'd first met her, he'd thought her weak, but he knew better now. She might be soft and subtle, but she was hardly weak. She was a tigress, and a worthy mate for his friend.

He turned away from the airstrip and nodded to his driver. For a man who had walked six miles through the jungle, he seemed surprisingly unfazed. The driver came around and opened the SUV door for him, and he got in, noting that the leather seats were as perfect and undisturbed as ever. The SUV had cost him nearly one hundred thousand dollars when all was said and done. Fully customized and capable of surviving a hail of bullets, this car was one of ten or twenty that he owned, spread out across the various countries and islands where he did his business. Like him, it was self-contained, holding everything he needed to survive and manage his empire.

For one brief moment he wondered what it would be like if he had met Sandra, if she had fallen in love with him instead of Sean. Of course, he had many women in his life. They fell all over him. After all, he was rich, powerful, relatively young and handsome.

He could snap his fingers and have any woman he wanted.

But he knew deep down inside that none of them were interested in him. They liked his money, his power. They found him sexy because he was dangerous. They giggled with their girlfriends over him and talked about him in hushed whispers. Briefly he found himself wishing that he had a woman like Sandra, a woman who would risk her life to stay with him. A woman interested in more than his money and power.

His cell phone rang and he picked it up automatically. It was his lieutenant, they'd found one of the spies. All business now, Valzar listened closely to the man's words, his mind spinning through possibilities and planning his next step.

As the SUV pulled away from the airstrip, he didn't give another thought to the wish he'd made just seconds earlier. Like so many of his wishes in life, it hung in the air behind him, left behind.

Just another forgotten wish . . .

DROP DEAD
SEXY

ELISA ADAMS

ONE

"IF YOU COULD DO anything in bed with a woman, what would it be?"

The keys slid from Nathan's hand and hit the ground with a clang of metal. His mouth went dry and his cock, never completely dormant around his drop-dead-sexy neighbor, went rock hard. A hundred ideas raced through his mind, half of which Joy had probably never even heard of. And the other half . . . *Jesus Christ.* If he told her what he wanted to do to a woman—to *her*—in bed, she'd never speak to him again. "Excuse me? Why would you even ask me that?"

"I'm just curious."

The sparkle in her blue eyes told him there was more to her question than simple curiosity. Seduction wasn't on her mind either, at least, he didn't think so, given the pajama shorts and tank top she wore and the messy ponytail she'd thrown her curly auburn hair into. Thank God for that. Most nights he simply avoided her, but tonight she'd managed to sneak up on him as he was coming home, throwing herself in his path and asking such an outrageous question that he couldn't help being intrigued.

He slumped against the wall and crossed his arms over his

chest, trying to think of a way to get rid of her. Intrigued or not, answering her question would only lead to problems he'd rather avoid. A sweet, innocent woman like his neighbor would run in the other direction if she knew what he'd want to do with a woman in bed. She wouldn't want to get caught up with someone like him. Would never understand his unusual needs. No matter how cute Joy was, she wasn't his type.

"That's an odd thing to be curious about." Though for her, he knew it wasn't. Every time they spoke, she had some sort of question for him. He supposed it went with the territory of living across the hall from a freelance journalist. The questions in the past had been simple, if not a little annoying, but they'd never even skirted the issue of sex until tonight. Tonight she'd changed the rules, and his body had sat up and taken notice in a big way. "What's really going on? Is this for work?"

She started to shake her head but then stopped and bit her lip. "Okay, so it's for work. Is that a crime?"

A sliver of disappointment worked its way into his mind, but he pushed it away. Why should he be irritated that she wasn't interested in him, just interested in picking his brain? He shouldn't be, but for some illogical reason he was. "Go home, Joy."

"Answer my question first." Her eyes narrowed and she raised her chin, and Nathan almost laughed. There was nothing tough about Joy Baker, no matter how much she tried to pretend there was. She was all sweetness and innocence wrapped up in a short, curvy package. The woman probably couldn't even kill a spider if she found one in her apartment. She could play tough all she wanted, but he wasn't buying it for a second.

"It's not a crime, but it could be dangerous to go around asking men you barely know what they like to do to women in bed." He lowered his voice to a near whisper. "You might end up getting more than you bargained for."

"Maybe I can handle a lot more than you think."

The thought made him swallow hard. So much for trying to chase her away. Now all he could think about was shoving her up against the wall, peeling off those insubstantial shorts and sinking his cock deep into her pussy.

Not that it would ever happen. In his experience, there were two types of people in the world when it came to sex—those who were adventurous and those who weren't. Joy looked like a straight-up missionary type of woman. The kind who tolerated sex and then rolled over and went to sleep. No way in hell could he deal with that, no matter how tempting those full lips were.

With a muttered curse, he bent and scooped his keys off the ground. He stood and unlocked the apartment door, suddenly needing to put some distance between them. A lot of distance. If he kept looking at her wearing next to nothing, breathing in her sweet scent of apples and flowers and warm, soft woman, he might just give her something she wasn't even asking for.

"Good night, Joy. Go home and get some sleep."

"Wait a second." Her fingers grasped the short sleeve of his T-shirt and she gave it a little tug. He tried to shake off the warmth that spread from his arm to all points in his body, but he couldn't quite manage it. "Can you please just give me five minutes of your time? I need your help."

Nathan leaned in and pressed his forehead to the doorjamb. Why now, of all times—With his family pushing him to do something he had no interest in—did she have to start asking provocative questions? They wanted him to find a nice woman and settle down. If his mother found out about Joy and his attraction to her, she'd never leave either of them alone. Now, with *settling down* the farthest thing from his mind, it wasn't the time to be getting involved with any woman, let alone one right across the hall.

"Shouldn't you be asleep?"

Images of Joy in bed flashed through his mind, and they didn't help his current situation. Joy naked, writhing on his sheets. Screaming his name as he—

Hell no. He needed to get inside before they both ended up in a heap of trouble.

"I'm writing an article for a women's magazine, and I've been researching. I heard you walking down the hall, and I thought having a live interview subject would be better than trying to weed through all the crap on the Internet."

He shook his head back and forth against the cool wood. "You're writing about what men want in bed?"

If so, that was an easy answer. He wanted Joy, completely bared to him, body and soul. On his bed, his couch, even on his fucking kitchen table. At this point, he wasn't in any state to be picky.

"The article is about how a woman can make her man's fantasies come true. Since I don't have a man of my own right now, I can't ask him what he'd want. I figured you, of all people, would understand sexual fantasies."

Now, wait a minute. What the hell was that supposed to mean? He turned around, his eyes narrowed. "Excuse me?"

Her shrug was casual enough, but the smug smile on her face told him she knew she'd gotten to him. "Just that I see you with a different woman every weekend."

"Just because I bring them here doesn't mean I sleep with them." *And even if I do, it's none of your business.* His family bothered him enough about his revolving girlfriends. Was there something wrong with a guy wanting to have a little fun before he was forced to settle down?

"It's always the middle of the night, and they're always all over you. Tell me you don't take them to bed."

The challenge written in her eyes brought a smile to his face. She'd noticed. That meant she'd been watching him as much as he'd been watching her. "Are you spying on me?"

"Of course not." She wrinkled her nose. "I'm a night person, usually awake watching TV when you bring your giggly, obnoxious girlfriends down the hallway. The walls around here are so thin I can practically hear what they're saying when they whisper in your ear."

Was that a hint of jealousy he detected in her voice? Nah. Couldn't be. She'd been avoiding him, and he'd been avoiding her.

Why had he been doing that again?

Because she wasn't. His. Type.

And if he repeated that a few thousand times, he might actually start to believe it. She *was* his type. *Exactly* his type, and his body had known it before his mind. But he'd be damned if he was going to be forced into something he wasn't ready for just because of some stupid tradition. He and his family had opposing views on lifetime commitment—they were all for it, and he preferred to pretend it didn't exist.

He blew out a breath. The situation was quickly moving into territory he'd rather not explore. At least not yet. In the two months since he'd moved in across the hall from her, they'd probably spoken a total of a hundred words to each other. This was the longest conversation they'd had to date, and yet he'd never really been able to get her off his mind. It was because he was a fucking fool, believing he could live across the hall from her, catch her scent in the air every day and not go out of his goddamned mind.

With a heavy sigh, he pushed away from the doorjamb. "Are you calling me a slut, Miss Baker?"

Humor sparked in her eyes. She raised her eyebrows but said nothing.

"And you think I'm willing to divulge my deepest, most secret fantasies to you so you can use them in some fluffy article for a *women's* magazine?"

"It would be anonymous. I wouldn't use your name or any iden-tifying details. Just the fantasies you're willing to share. I'm not writing erotica. It's just an article. What's the harm in answering a couple of stupid questions?"

The questions posed no problem. It was what they might lead to that bothered him. "Okay. You want to ask questions, who am I to stop you?"

"You'll help me?"

He nodded. As if she'd given him any choice. He'd help, but it would come with a price. He'd kept his distance from her. Until tonight. Now she wanted to change the way their relationship—or lack thereof—worked, and he had a feeling nothing he could say would dissuade her. He'd been a gentleman. Until now. The second she walked over the threshold into his apartment, all bets were off. "Better get inside quick, before I change my mind."

If he could keep his hands off her for five minutes, they'd both be lucky. At this rate, three minutes without touching her would be a freakin' miracle.

After only a second's hesitation, she scooted inside and he fol-lowed, closing the door behind them. He switched on the light by the door and turned to face her. The second her gaze snagged his, the room seemed to shrink to the size of a postage stamp. He couldn't tear his eyes away, and each second passed like an eternity.

He swallowed against the dryness in his throat. If he hadn't been sure before, he was now. He was a goner.

Joy glanced away, her gaze taking in his plain white-walled apartment, and he cleared his throat. "You want a beer or something?"

"No, thanks. I don't drink."

"Water? Coffee?"

"Thanks anyway. I'm all set. Nervous about something?"

Nervous? No. Horny and ready to jump all over her was more like it. That and a few other things he wouldn't even allow himself to think about. It would be best to keep his thoughts on track for now or risk spilling his whole story. She'd have to know soon, but not yet. If he told her now, she'd think he was some kind of deranged stalker.

Time to focus on the more immediate matter of Joy's question. What he would want to do with a woman in bed.

What the hell did she want from him, anyway? Women didn't really want to know about men's fantasies, did they? Of course not. They wanted a glazed-over, sweetened version that wouldn't make them feel guilty in the morning. Why would Joy be any different?

"I have nothing to be nervous about. I'm just trying to be a good host." A host to a woman he wanted out of his apartment and out of his mind before she caused permanent damage to his carefully ordered life.

She laughed then—a rich, husky sound that sent heat spiraling through his gut. It settled in his cock and made him harder than before. *Shit.* Why wouldn't she just go home? Just talking about his fantasies was going to make him think of all the things he wanted to do to her. Things she would never let him do.

Fuck this. Keeping his distance wasn't working. Maybe scaring her would send her packing and he could get on with his life. If not, they both had to live with the consequences.

"I could tell you all about my fantasies," he started, moving across the carpet toward her. "But I'd rather show you. Firsthand experience is always the best way to learn."

TWO

*J*OY'S JAW DROPPED. WAS he kidding? Her gaze flew to his jeans and the impressive bulge she found there. Her panties went damp. Okay, so he wasn't kidding. Go figure. He'd never hinted at being interested before. She'd always thought her complete and total lust for the guy was one-sided, but apparently she'd been wrong.

She licked her lips and took a deep breath, trying to calm her suddenly raging hormones. She hadn't anticipated this. This was *so* not a place she wanted to be tonight. All she'd wanted was to finish her article. Well, almost all. . . . Still, deadlines needed to come before men, no matter how tempting the man was. "Not a good idea. You're not really my type."

It was a total lie, but she'd never admit it to the man.

"How do you know that? We've barely even spoken before."

"I just want to ask you a few questions. I'm not looking for a one-night stand."

"So ask." He took a step closer and then another until he stood only a few inches away. Her whole body took notice. Her fingers itched to thread through all that dark hair. She wanted to feel him.

Wanted to taste him. Did he really expect her to ask him questions now, with him standing so close?

As if she could even form a coherent thought with so much testosterone filling the air around them. This was exactly why she normally avoided men like Nathan Halloran—they were more trouble than they were worth. It would be best to stick to the subject for her article tonight. Men's fantasies and how women can fulfill them.

Damned if she didn't want to fulfill all of his, right that second.

"Okay, answer my first question. The one I asked right before you dropped your keys."

"What would I want to do with a woman in bed? Sweetheart, most of my fantasies don't even involve a bed. I can think of a lot of other places where I'd rather have fun."

Her panties dampened even more and her nipples poked against the soft fabric of the tank top. Her body swayed toward him and if she hadn't caught herself in time, she would have ended up draped against that hard chest. What had she gotten herself into? Thinking Nathan could help her with her research might have been a bit of a mistake. Suddenly a simple interview wasn't going to work for her anymore. Now that he'd made the suggestion to show her, she wanted to find out his fantasies in a much more physical manner. "Would you care to elaborate?"

"The weather is nice this time of year." He glanced toward the sliding door leading out to the small balcony identical to hers. "Don't you think?"

"You like to do it outside? In *public*?"

"Sometimes. It mixes things up a little so life doesn't get boring."

She didn't care for boring, but she couldn't do something that

would get her arrested either. *That* would lead to too many questions she didn't want to answer. "I would hardly think sleeping
with a different person every Friday night would get boring."

"Trust me. It does."

The sincerity in his tone resonated somewhere inside her.
She didn't have to take his word for it. She knew. She'd sworn
off men—and sex—for that very reason months ago. Up until
tonight, she hadn't even missed it. Much.

Instead of prying into his personal life, she made one last
attempt to keep things as professional as they could be, given that
she'd ambushed him in his hallway minutes earlier. "Talk to me,
Nathan. Tell me what it is that men *really* want."

"Are you sure you want the answer to that?"

"My career might depend on it." This article was big. Huge. Or
at least it had the potential to be. It could make or break her bud-
ding career and at this stage in her life, the thought of searching
for a job in another field made her head ache. Been there, done
that, had the lousy paycheck stubs to prove it.

Nathan laughed. The deep sound of it made her toes curl and
she delighted in the little shiver that ran through her. He wasn't
her type, and that fact drew her to him even more. She usually preferred sleek, stylish men in designer suits. Polished men. Nathan
was far from polished and at first she'd wondered what the bevy
of women he brought home saw in him, but it wasn't long before
she'd figured it out. There was something about him that made
it impossible to look away. His features were a little rough, his
appearance a little less than perfect, but all in all, the package was
so unbelievably sexy that she couldn't help being drawn in.

"Okay. What men really want." His smile was nothing short
of sinful. "Just remember, you asked for it. Most men need visual
stimulation. They like to see a woman in sexy lingerie. Like to

see her doing sexy things. Dancing or stripping, or even eating can be a huge turn-on if she's making it sexy. Words aren't really important most of the time. I know you don't want to hear this, but emotions usually aren't either. The visuals are."

"So you don't like a woman to talk dirty to you?" The question was out before she could stop it. She gave herself a mental kick in the butt for egging him on. She was there for research, not to get laid, no matter how much the latter appealed to her deprived body.

"I didn't say that at all. I just said it wasn't a necessity. Now *this* is another story." He flicked the strap of her tank top and it slid off her shoulder, revealing the top curve of her breast. His gaze dropped down and lingered, heat flashing in his eyes. "Walking into a room and seeing you like this would get me hard in about two seconds."

She put the strap back in place, her face flaming. Up until that moment, she'd forgotten that she'd run out of her apartment in her pajamas. She'd been so eager to talk to him that she hadn't even realized how indecent she must look. At least she had shorts on this time. Most nights she slept in just a tank top and underwear. "Oh really."

She tried to keep her tone casual, but the look in his eyes when he raised his gaze back to hers told her she'd failed.

"A lot of men like women who are bold in bed, who aren't afraid to tell a man what they want. But at the same time, it can be a huge turn-on if a woman lets the man dictate what's going to happen and when. If she gives herself over to him and lets him take care of her pleasure." A sensual smile stretched his lips. "What do you want, Joy? What do *you* like in bed?"

Crap. At the moment, she didn't care. Anything he wanted would be fine. She just wanted something to ease the ache that

had started the second Nathan had dragged her into his apartment. "Uh . . ."

"Do you like the man you're with to decide for you? To take
charge?"

Not usually, but something about Nathan made that idea seem
like the best one she'd heard in a long time. She opened her mouth
to deny his claim, but nothing came out.

"What's the matter? Aren't you going to answer me?"

He stepped closer and reached out to grasp a strand of her
hair. Standing this close to him, she got her first good look at his
eyes. They were green. A deep mossy color threaded with golden
flecks. His hair was dark, the color of espresso, and it hung to his
shoulders. Up until she stood so close to him, she hadn't realized
how tall he was. Probably around six foot two, though almost all
men looked tall from where she stood at five foot three.

"This isn't about what I want."

"Isn't it?" He gave the strand of hair a tug and she moved forward, her bare toes bumping into his boots. Nathan laughed and
dropped her hair, his finger trailing down the side of her cheek to
her neck. Joy swallowed hard and tried to back away, but his free
hand grasped her arm and held her near him while he continued
his exploration.

His finger dipped lower, down the side of her neck, before
he brought it down and circled her nipple through the fabric of
her top. The nub of flesh went even harder and she let out a little
sound of surprise.

"No. This is about what *men* want. If it was about me, I wouldn't
have needed to bother you with questions."

"Oh really?" He leaned in and nipped at her neck, sending a
riot of sensation through her core. The feel of the man's teeth
against her skin drove her wild. Almost out of their own volition,

her hands came up and grabbed his shoulders, her fingers digging into the soft material of his shirt. "Is that all this is about? An article?"

Not even close. "Well, it's certainly not your stellar charms."

That got another laugh out of him. "You haven't been interested, even a little bit?" His tongue grazed the side of her neck and her fingers tightened against his arms. "'Cause I've been interested in you."

"Why didn't you ever say anything?"

"You're not my type." His mouth closed over her earlobe and he nibbled on the sensitive flesh.

A tremor raced through her pussy. Her back arched. "What exactly is your type?"

Her lobe left his mouth with a pop and he straightened up, dislodging her hands from his shoulders as he moved a few inches away from her. He stared at her for a long time, eyes narrowed, before he spoke in a low whisper. "It's hard to explain. I just know that you're not it. But at the same time, something makes me think you are."

"That makes no sense."

"Tell me about it." He shook his head and seemed to shake off the confusion filling his gaze at the same time. When he looked at her again, it was with nothing but heat and lust and something undefined that made her pussy quiver again. He moved back and flopped onto the couch, his legs stretched out in front of him and his hands clasped behind his head. "Take off your shirt, sweetheart."

Sweetheart? Was he kidding? "I'm not one of your fan club."

A short chuckle followed her denial. "I'm aware of that. Actually, I'm very aware of everything about you. Take off your shirt and let me see those amazing breasts."

The deep, hypnotic quality in his voice sent a shiver through her. Her body begged for her to listen to him, to do as he asked in hopes of getting a little relief from the frustration she'd felt for so long. If anyone could relieve the bone-deep boredom that had settled in, it was Nathan and this little game he was playing. If she had to admit the truth, she'd wanted him for too long to deny herself the pleasure of finally having him. He wanted an obedient woman? Fine. She could manage that. For a little while. Her turn would come next.

"Afraid of something?" The taunting in his voice prodded her to move. Her fingers found the hem of her tank top and she pulled it over her head. A second later the soft material dropped to the floor at her feet.

Nathan said nothing, but his eyes darkened even more. He licked his lips.

Goose bumps broke out over her skin, and they had nothing to do with a chill in the air. His scrutiny seemed to go on forever. The intensity in his gaze made her every muscle clench tight. Her nipples were so hard they ached.

"Touch them for me," he said in a low growl. "I want to watch you play with your nipples."

Her hands shaking, she brought them up and cupped her breasts. She flicked her thumbs across her nipples and moaned from the sparks the contact ignited.

"Pinch them," he told her.

"Why don't you?"

A deep chuckle vibrated through the room. "Come over here and I will."

When she didn't move, he raised his eyebrows. "Come over here and sit in my lap, Joy."

Her gaze dropped down to his lap and the bulge of his cock

straining against his jeans. She licked her lips. He didn't have to tell her twice. She walked over to the couch, straddled his legs and lowered herself down until her pussy rested against that bulge. The urge to rub herself against him was strong, but she held back, wanting to see what Nathan had in mind.

She expected him to touch the breasts he'd been staring at since she'd stripped off her top, but he didn't. Instead he leaned in and captured her lips.

The kiss was deep, possessive, his tongue probing the recesses of her mouth. His fingers threaded through her hair and he tilted her head to deepen the kiss. She moaned against his lips. It had been forever since someone had kissed her like that. Like she was the only woman in the world he'd ever wanted.

Heat started low in her stomach and spiraled out to her limbs. Her lips tingled. Her fingers dug into his shoulders as she held on tight, reveling in every sensation he stirred inside her.

Her back arched, forcing her bare breasts against his chest. Her nipples rubbed against the fabric of his shirt and she cried out, the sensations almost too much to take. She needed so much more than a kiss. Needed it soon.

He broke the contact and trailed his tongue down her neck until he reached her breasts. In the next second, his hands cupped her breasts and he plumped them together. He leaned down and bit one of her nipples.

A gasp caught in her throat. "What are you doing?"

"Let me worry about that. I don't want you to talk anymore. Don't speak. Feel. You just relax and enjoy."

Like she could relax right now with every cell in her body screaming for him to get closer. "Nathan?"

Without warning he dropped his hands and sat back. His eyebrows rose. "What?"

She didn't have an answer, so she said nothing. She'd rather wait and see how the whole thing played out.

She let out a deep breath. "This is nuts."

"No. You asking me questions like the one you asked a few minutes ago is nuts. This is probably the only sane thing I've done in a long time. This is a two-way street. I'm willing to help you, but you've got to do something for me too."

"So this is your fantasy? Doing it sitting up on a couch? I have to say, I'm a little disappointed."

The smile dropped from her face when she got a good look at his eyes. For the first time in a long time, she realized she was in deep trouble.

His low chuckle reverberated around her. "This isn't my fantasy. Not even close."

"Then what is it?"

He didn't answer, but the look in his eyes told her all she needed to know. She was in so much trouble now.

Finally. It was about damned time too.

THREE

*J*OY SQUIRMED AGAINST THE hard seat of the chair. Nathan's fantasy was one she hadn't expected. One she hadn't even realized would be a turn-on, but she'd never been so wet in her life.

Once he'd stripped her of the rest of her clothes, he'd brought in a chair from the kitchen and told her to sit. She hadn't been prepared for what he'd done after that. Even now she was still shocked at the way she'd let him bind her ankles to the chair legs and tie her arms behind her back. She was naked, completely open and bared to him, and though the black silk scarf he'd tied around her eyes prevented her from seeing him, she could feel his heated gaze raking every inch of her body.

"Nathan?" She squirmed again, trying to get some relief from the incredible tension thrumming through her body. Going without sex for months had been a mistake. How could he possibly expect her to sit there like this when she was about to come out of her skin?

"Don't speak. Don't move."

He wanted her to hold still? She snorted. That wasn't even possible. "I can't help it. I'm going crazy here."

"We had this discussion already, Joy." This time he whispered in her ear. His hot breath fanned her cheek and she shivered. "You need to be quiet or I'll leave you like this until you are."

He brought his hands to her breasts, but instead of cupping them this time, he pinched her nipples between his thumbs and forefingers. The rough touch sent a spark of heat through her core, settling into a rush of moisture in her pussy.

Something inside warned her that he meant it, and she needed to learn, if only for tonight, to keep her big mouth shut. Her mouth had gotten her into trouble more times than she could count, but she wasn't about to let one of those times be tonight. She wasn't about to pass up what might be a once-in-a-lifetime opportunity.

"You asked me what my fantasy is," he continued, his tone pure sin. Gone was the easygoing, laid-back neighbor she'd known for months. In his place was a strong, self-assured man who made her whole body throb for release. "Right now, right here with you, this is what I want. Can you give me that?"

She debated asking him to untie her for all of two seconds, but in the end her body won out over her mind.

"Yes." For one night. After that, she'd have to take matters into her own hands.

NATHAN WATCHED JOY FOR her reaction, and he was a little bit surprised when she didn't fight him. Instead she nodded, and his cock went rock hard. Part of him had been trying to chase her away, to make her see that she was nuts asking him to tell her anything, let alone his wildest fantasies.

The woman had no clue what she'd started. None. This wasn't his *wildest* fantasy. Far from it. But it was tame enough that he could share it with her without revealing too much about himself. There were things innocent little Joy wouldn't want to know.

Then again, maybe she wasn't as innocent as he'd first thought.

He glanced her over, taking in the flushed pink color of her skin, the way her nipples were pebbled, her parted lips and the way her tongue swiped across them from time to time.

And her pussy. Her lower lips glistened with her juices and he licked his lips. For two months, since he'd moved in across the hall, he'd been dying to get a taste of her. Tonight, he would finally get his chance. She'd all but dumped herself into his lap tonight and though he'd spent the better part of the past few weeks trying to ignore what he already knew, he couldn't do it anymore. Her little stunt had taken the choice out of his hands. With her so close, so open and naked, he intended to take full advantage.

Without a word to her, he left the room and went into his bedroom and rummaged through the bottom drawer of his dresser until he found what he was looking for. *Perfect.* She wanted a fantasy, and he'd give her one. By the time he finished with her, she wouldn't even be able to walk.

It FELT LIKE AN eternity had passed since Nathan had left her sitting there, and in another five seconds Joy was going to tell him to take his fantasies and shove them. She could write the article without him and this waiting crap. It was one thing to tie her up and blindfold her. It was something she hadn't tried before, but she could get into it. Leaving her all alone was something totally different. It had been his idea that they act out his fantasies rather than her just writing down what he said, so why was he doing this?

In the next instant, she got her answer as a faint buzzing sound filled the room, along with Nathan's heavy, booted footsteps.

"Nathan?" She swallowed hard and licked her lips. "What are you doing?"

He didn't answer. Instead the buzzing grew louder and she heard his footsteps as he walked across the room toward her. She knew that buzzing sound. Heard a similar one every time she switched on one of her vibrators. What did he have planned? The possibilities made her mouth water.

His hand came down on her shoulder and she shifted on the chair. "Hold still, Joy. I want to make this good for you, but I can't if you won't listen to me."

A scathing reply waited on the tip of her tongue, but she held it back. She could lay into him for his domineering attitude later. Right now she was having too much fun to protest. To think, a few months ago she'd looked at all men as boring. Nathan had quickly made her see how wrong she'd been in that assumption.

The vibrator brushed across the curve of her breast and she shivered. A second later, it brushed her nipple. She arched her back into the touch, the sensations made a hundred times stronger since she couldn't see what he was doing. Couldn't move more than a few inches in any direction. She tugged at the ties holding her arms behind her back, but they wouldn't budge.

Nathan's deep chuckle filled her senses. He dragged the vibrator from one breast to the other and back again, teasing her nipples until he was driving her wild. She'd never been so hot for a man before. Any man. And in her life, there had been more than a few. None of them were able to do for her in weeks what Nathan had managed in less than an hour. Why had she thought sleeping with him would be a bad idea?

If there had ever been a valid reason, she couldn't remember what it was now.

The vibrator left her skin, but the buzzing didn't stop. Soon she felt Nathan's palms on her thighs, spreading her legs even more. She let out a soft moan.

"When a woman is blindfolded," he whispered into her ear, "all her other senses are heightened."

Didn't she know it. Every touch seemed to sear her skin. His scent, crisp and masculine, filled the air around her. She heard his every movement, every breath and it made her feel in tune with him in a way that was foreign to her. It should have made her nervous, but instead it only made her hotter. The buzzing sound stopped, throwing the room into silence, and she sat up a little straighter. What did he have planned now?

The vibrator touched her lips and she flinched out of surprise.

"Suck it, Joy. Get it nice and wet for your pussy."

Her pussy didn't need any added lubrication, but when she opened her mouth to tell him that, he slipped the toy between her lips.

"That is so fucking hot. Do you know how beautiful you look to me right now?"

His murmured words spurred her on. She bobbed her head up and down the length of the vibrator, swirling her tongue over the head with each upstroke, hoping she was teasing him as much as he was teasing her. His soft groan let her know she was, and the thought made her smile.

Soon Nathan pulled the toy from her lips and the buzzing sound filled the room again. Her whole body tensed, her pussy softening in anticipation. He trailed the vibrator down her stomach, stopping to tease her skin at various points, before he brought it between her legs to stroke across her clit.

She clenched her hands into fists, her lips parting on a moan. Her breathing was heavy, jagged, and her throat had gone bone dry. Her nipples ached and the muscles of her pussy quivered.

Three strokes of that toy across her clit were all it took for her body to explode into orgasm.

She rocked back and forth, her body only able to move a few inches. It was frustrating and stimulating at the same time—like nothing she'd ever felt before. Everything dissolved into light and sensation and she could barely catch her breath. Still he continued to tease her sensitive flesh, alternating between hard and soft touches, drawing the toy away only to press it back against her again.

The chair rocked with her movements as he took her farther and farther from her comfort zone, making her cry out and scream his name—and he had yet to actually touch her.

After what felt like an eternity, her breathing started to return to normal and she slumped against the bonds, waiting for Nathan to release her.

He didn't.

Instead, he brought the vibrator lower, trailing it over her sensitized folds until he reached the entrance to her cunt. He pushed it inside, sending another round of tremors through her body.

"Oh my God." Her muscles gripped the smooth surface of the vibrator and she bucked her hips against it. Nathan found her clit and he pinched it lightly between his thumb and forefinger. Sensation zinged from the spot out to her limbs, making her body tingle from head to toe. It seemed like she hung in limbo for an eternity, her movements uncontrolled and her eyes closed. The only thing she could focus on was Nathan and how he was making her feel.

By the time she came back to earth, her wrists and ankles had gone numb from straining against the bonds.

Nathan pulled the toy out of her, and soon after, the buzzing stopped. She thought he would move away but he didn't. Instead she felt his tongue trail a hot, wet line up the inside of her thigh.

"Nathan, stop."

He stilled but nipped the tender skin of her outer lip. "You want this."

"I can't take any more. Twice is enough."

His laughter rumbled against her. "You can handle more."

His tongue dipped between her legs and swirled over her clit. It was the most amazing thing she'd felt in a long time and she canted her hips forward as much as she could, eager for more. The orgasm started over, building and building until her body burst into sensation. Her mind shut down and she could do nothing except rock against him, alternately screaming his name and begging him not to stop. The tremors seemed to go on forever, and when he finally pulled his mouth away, her head dropped back, limp.

Nathan untied her and helped her stand, and he took off the blindfold.

She shivered at the look in his eyes. "That was your fantasy?" she asked, her voice barely above a whisper. Every now and then a delicious errant tremor raced through her.

He just shook his head and let out a sensual laugh.

"What's so funny?"

He leaned in and brushed a kiss across the side of her neck. "Yeah, that was one of my biggest fantasies—at least where you're involved."

"You've had fantasies about me before?"

He raised his eyebrows before nodding his head. "Every day. Does that surprise you?"

"Actually, yes." And it thrilled her too. He'd been thinking about her. It sent a little shiver straight to her toes.

She'd been thinking about him too. Too much. She'd never admit it to him though.

"You know what another of my biggest fantasies about you is?" Nathan asked.

Somehow, she didn't think they were talking about the article anymore. Surprisingly, she was okay with that.

He smiled at her and she shook right down to her toes.

Maybe a little more than okay.

"What?"

"I'll have to show you sometime. It's pretty simple, actually." The way his smile grew told her it was anything but.

FOUR

*N*ATHAN'S COCK FELT READY to burst. If he didn't get inside Joy—now—he had a feeling he might explode. She was spent, probably wouldn't be able to stand for long, let alone hold herself up for what he had in mind. Instead, he took her hand and led her out the sliding door onto the small balcony. The cool night air brushed his skin but did nothing to ease the heat coursing through him. The woman was incredible. Why hadn't he seen it before?

He shook his head. He *had* seen it. That was why he'd avoided her for so long. He should still be avoiding her, rather than walking right into something he swore he never even wanted. He should, but he couldn't. With Joy this close, the lure was too strong to resist. He needed to keep her off balance by keeping her guessing, allowing him to stay in control for a little longer. If he let her see how she affected him yet, she'd run away before he got the chance to explain things. She wouldn't understand.

Panic raced across her gaze for a second, and he couldn't help leaning in to press a hard, fast kiss on her lips. She really was beautiful. Not in a conventional way, but in every way that mattered. He responded to her in ways he'd tried to deny for too long. As much as it aggravated him, it was well past time to stop denying.

In all honesty, *where* he had her didn't even matter anymore, just that it happened. But she wanted fantasies and he didn't mind giving them to her. Especially if it would keep her from learning the truth for a little bit longer. *That* confession was one he didn't want to make until it was absolutely necessary.

He stepped back and leaned against the wooden railing that overlooked the courtyard two stories below. "Are you okay with this?"

She cocked her head to the side, her eyes still glazed with remnants of lust. "Let me get this straight. The first fantasy was about tying a woman to a chair and making her come while you're still dressed?"

"No. That was a personal fantasy, not something that every man wants. I've wanted to have you helpless for a long time."

Her eyes darkened, and a shiver ran through her. Her nipples peaked again and he barely resisted the urge to put his mouth on them. That would come in time. Now there were more important things he needed to do. She was his. He'd known it the second he'd seen her, but he'd refused to admit it. Now he couldn't deny it and he needed to show her where she belonged.

"Aren't you worried about someone seeing us?" she asked, her tone uncertain. "This is a pretty big apartment complex."

"It's two in the morning. I don't think that'll be a problem."

She didn't protest further. Instead she walked over to him, cupped his face in her hand and kissed him long and deep. She brought her other hand between them to caress his cock through the material of his jeans. Soon the first hand joined the second and, before he could protest, she'd unzipped his pants, freed his cock and was circling the hard length of him in the heat of her palm.

Nathan broke the kiss and sucked in a breath. "If you keep touching me like that, I'm not going to last."

As it was, he'd been on edge since he'd tied her to the chair. He'd been fighting the urge to give up the whole fantasy angle, to bend her forward over the chair and ram into her for too long. Now she was touching him and his control was making a hasty retreat.

"You don't want to come?" The smile on her face told him she had revenge on her mind and he swallowed hard. "I'm very well sated, Nathan. I'm really not worried about how long you'll last."

"I thought this was supposed to be about my fantasies?"

She dropped to her knees in front of him. "It is."

In the next second, she'd slid her mouth over his cock and was bobbing her head up and down along the length. He let out a hard groan and tightened his hold on the railing behind him. She was an expert, and if she kept going he'd come before he even got inside her. That was the last thing he wanted.

She cupped his balls in one hand, giving them a gentle squeeze, while she continued to work his cock. Lost in the feel of her all around him, he closed his eyes and let his head drop back until she groaned against him. He looked down, shocked to find she'd slipped a hand between her legs. This turned her on as much as it did him. He smiled at the thought.

As much as he wanted her to continue, though, he couldn't let that happen tonight. Though she had an incredible mouth, he'd much rather come in her pussy. He nudged her head away, helped her stand and bent her over one of the wicker chairs on the deck. Her hands hit the surface, her ass coming up in the air. His smile widened. He'd give anything to sink his teeth into the skin of that full, rounded ass. *Anything.* So he did.

He leaned down and nipped at the tender skin just above her

hip. She rewarded him with a harsh groan, her body pitching forward. "What are you doing?"

"Sorry. I couldn't help myself. You taste so good."

She laughed, but the sound was strained.

"You don't like biting?" he asked, only half teasing.

"Just the opposite. I like it too much."

Something told him they'd get along just fine.

His cock ached, more than ready to be satisfied, and he couldn't hold back any longer. He pressed it against her wet cunt, holding himself still for a few seconds before pushing inside. He didn't stop until he was fully seated. Joy was a tight fit and it thrilled him to think she could take all of him. Her muscles clamped down on him and he shuddered.

She squirmed back against him, prodding him to move. Though he tried to keep his strokes slow and measured, that didn't last long. Soon he couldn't do anything more than hold her hips in place while he pounded into her, relishing every hard stroke. Joy deserved gentle, easy loving after what he'd done earlier, but she wasn't going to get it tonight. Now that he was inside her, his mind started to shut down. He needed her so badly. Had for so long. He couldn't even think straight. The only thing he knew now was her scent and the feel of her hugging him so tight.

Mine.

The thought came out of nowhere, surprising him, but he didn't deny it. Couldn't. It was a fact that had slapped him in the face the second he'd gotten a whiff of that luscious feminine scent.

He reached around and fingered her clit, knowing from her soft exhales and the tremors racing through her that she was close. He owed it to her not to leave her hanging. Once he found his own release, it would be a while before he had the strength to go at it again.

The woman wanted a fantasy? He nearly laughed. She had no idea what she'd gotten herself into with him. Some of his fantasies might very well be her worst nightmares.

He wouldn't think about that now though. She didn't need to know anything more about him just yet.

His balls drew up tight against his body. If he counted to ten, over and over, maybe he could last. Just when he thought he couldn't take another second, Joy cried out his name and her inner muscles convulsed around him. The feel of her orgasm gave him the final push over the edge. The fingers of his free hand tight on her hip, he stroked hard into her as his release washed over him, threatening to tear him apart with its intensity. It was ages before he could think again, let alone move.

If he hadn't been sure about what she meant to him before, he was now, and that scared him more than anything.

FIVE

OY ZIPPED UP HER skirt. She had made plans to go out for a quick bite with a few friends and was just about ready to go when someone knocked on her apartment door. She glanced in the peephole and saw Nathan standing in the hall.

"Shit," she muttered. For the past few days, since she'd run out on him in the middle of the night, she'd been trying to think of a way to explain to him what had happened. How could she explain it when she didn't even understand it herself? She unlocked the door and pulled it open a crack. Just the sight of him, standing there in worn jeans and a T-shirt, his feet bare, made her mouth water. Her nipples pebbled, and there was no way she could hide her reaction. All he'd have to do was look down at her thin, tight shirt and he'd know. "Hi."

"Hi yourself."

His smile did funny things to her insides. Things she tried to ignore. Ever since she'd left him sleeping in his bed after the night they'd shared, she'd been trying to put what had happened aside, knowing it would be best for both of them. So far, it wasn't working. Seeing him only made her body—and her heart—ache. "What's going on?"

"I wanted to talk to you for a little while."

Not a good idea. *So* not a good idea. "I'm actually leaving right now. Meeting friends downtown. Can we talk tomorrow?"

"Come on, Joy. It'll only take a second."

She sighed and stepped back to let him in. Might as well get it over with. He was probably going to tell her he never wanted to see her again, that what had happened between them had been a mistake brought on by her unusual questions. They'd gotten carried away. The thought should have eased her mind, but for some reason it didn't.

"What's up?" She tried to plaster a bright smile on her face. No sense getting worked up over a one-night stand. And that's really all they'd had, despite her mind's insistence that something more had gone on between them.

The second she had the door closed, he pressed her up against it and kissed her.

She parted her lips in surprise and he delved his tongue inside, thrusting deep. His hands gripped her hips, pulling her tight against him as he continued his exploration of the recesses of her mouth. She held on tight, her head spinning and her world tilting on its axis. So maybe he hadn't come to tell her he didn't want to see her again. A giggle welled up inside her, quickly followed by a burst of heat. Damn, the man felt so good. It had only been two days, but somehow it felt like an eternity. Everything inside her ached for him. Maybe always had.

When he broke the kiss, she could barely remember her name. After clearing her throat and taking a few deep breaths, she was finally able to speak again. "I thought you said you wanted to talk?"

"I lied."

"So there isn't something you need to talk to me about?"

"No. Not now. Later." He didn't give her a chance to respond before he hiked her skirt up to her waist and lifted one of her legs around his hips. He ground his cock against her. His lips dipped down to the spot where her neck met her collar. His movements were fast, erratic, and her pussy got wet at the roughness of his touch. He wasn't smooth, but she liked him that way.

"Nathan?"

He glanced up at her long enough to shake his head. "Later." His hands tugged at her panties, pulling at them until the material tore away from her skin. A second later the scrap of fabric dropped to the floor. His intensity should have made her nervous, but for some reason it only increased her arousal. She tugged at his shirt, eager to get it off his body.

He didn't give her a chance to look him over. Soon he lifted her other leg around his hip and he was inside her, stroking into her with a ferocity that slammed her back against the door. Half out of her mind with lust, she leaned forward and kissed the side of his neck. His moan encouraged her and he pulled her down against him, thrusting harder inside her. The orgasm that followed took her by surprise, stealing her breath.

Her lips tight on his neck, she bit down as her orgasm spiraled through her, aware of the fact that Nathan's teeth had sunk into her shoulder. The sharp pain made her gasp. Her fingers dug into his shoulders and she held on tight, riding the waves along with him as his own release washed over him.

When he set her down on her feet, her whole body felt liquid.

"What time are you supposed to meet your friends?" he asked, his breathing as heavy as hers.

Was he kidding? No way was she walking away from him now.

"I'm not going. Suddenly I'm not feeling very hungry anymore." At least not for food. "Can you stay tonight?"

The smile on his face told her he would.

"WHY DID YOU WALK out the other night?" Nathan stroked the flat of his palm down Joy's side, loving the little shiver that ran through her when he got to her hip. She was ticklish, and it made him smile.

She rolled onto her side and kissed him—a long, leisurely kiss full of affection but not lust. After he'd nearly attacked her against her front door, they'd moved to the bed and spent a good few hours getting to know each other a lot better. No clothes, no fantasies between them. Just the two of them. It was a scene that normally would have made him uncomfortable, but with her, it felt almost . . . right.

"I don't know why I left. It was too intense, I guess. I wasn't looking for anything permanent."

"Have you changed your mind now?"

A small smile graced her full lips. "Maybe. I guess we'll just have to wait and see."

"You scare me. Do you know that?"

She blinked. "Why would I scare you?"

"It's hard to explain. This just feels so right. It shouldn't so soon."

"Then I guess we'll have to spend some time exploring the possibilities." Her lips parted in a yawn. "But not now. I need to catch a few hours first."

He leaned in to her neck and drew a deep breath of her rich, heady scent. It would be forever imprinted on his mind after tonight. Somehow the thought didn't make him nearly as nervous as he thought it should.

Nathan wandered into the kitchen, parched and in need of a drink. It was an odd feeling, being so thirsty that he was afraid a simple glass of water wouldn't do. After the workout she'd put him through though, it made sense. He hadn't even had a chance to have dinner before he'd gone to see her the night before, and they certainly hadn't taken a break for something as time-consuming as a meal.

He yawned and stretched, his mind flashing back to the night with Joy. It had been amazing. No pretenses, no articles or questions to get in the way. Just the two of them and hot, freakin' incredible sex. And talking. He'd never been one for much talking before, but he found he wanted to get to know her better on more than just the carnal level. He could really get used to her being around. The thought would have scared him once, but now it only made him think of the possibilities.

He opened the fridge, his eyes still bleary, but the only things he found inside turned his stomach. Blood bags. Lots of them. *What the fuck?*

He stood up and slammed the fridge closed, his fingers going to his neck and the spot she'd bitten the night before. Two tiny raised lumps alerted him to what he probably should have suspected a lot sooner. Would have suspected, had he not been so wrapped up in denying that he wanted her.

How in the hell had this happened?

"Nathan?"

He spun to find Joy standing in the doorway, wrapped in the sheet they'd torn off the bed.

"Why do you have a fridge full of blood?" And why the fuck had he *not known?*

"I can explain."

His knees buckled and he had to lean back against the counter. Somehow he doubted he'd like her explanation.

Given the recent discovery, she'd like his confession even less.

SIX

OY STOOD IN THE door, blocking Nathan's only escape from the kitchen. She couldn't let him leave now. Not until she'd had a chance to explain. If he ran out of here now, all kinds of trouble would happen.

"You're a vampire."

It wasn't a question but a statement instead. She nodded, frowning at the fact that he didn't look at her like she was nuts. He looked shocked but not altogether surprised.

"For real?" He gave a little nervous laugh that seemed to be out of character. "No way. This can't be happening. I don't do vampires."

Not really the reaction she'd been expecting. Or the one she'd been hoping for. Since their first night together she'd envisioned the moment he found out over and over in her head, playing out all the possible scenarios. This one hadn't even made the list. "What are you talking about?"

"Exactly what I said. I don't *do* vampires."

"Excuse me?"

He pushed away from the counter and paced the length of the kitchen, running his hand through his dark hair. His jeans rode low on his hips, revealing a tantalizing amount of skin below. Suddenly he stopped and faced her, his eyes narrowed. "You bit me."

"Sorry. I'd planned on going out to feed last night, but you sort of got in the way."

"You probably shouldn't have done that."

"I said I was sorry. I didn't take much. Just enough to get me through the night. You bit me too. Pretty hard, I might add."

"And that's exactly what the problem is. If I'd known about your little issue, I never would have done that."

He made it sound like she'd deliberately kept something from him. Well, she had, but not because she didn't want him to know. Because she'd been afraid of his reaction. Most humans would have laughed and told her to find psychiatric help. "What are you talking about?"

"I'm a werewolf."

Her stomach bottomed out and she had to lean against the door frame for support. *Oh shit.* This couldn't be happening. "You're a what?" Her voice came out as nothing more than a squeak.

"A werewolf. You know, all furry and howling at the moon?" He took a few steps closer but then seemed to change his mind and backed up again. "Do you know it only takes a bite from a werewolf to become one? Just one bite. It's the saliva that does it. All it takes is a little bit."

She whimpered. Her breath caught in her lungs and she had to pound her fist on her chest to get it back. "Why did you bite me so hard?"

"I didn't mean to, damn it. You bit me first, and instinct kicked in and I sort of went out of my mind."

"You couldn't control yourself?" Something in the way he said those words thrilled her. She made him lose control. How long had she waited to hear that from a man?

Okay, so it was very possible that the man had turned her into a werewolf, but the idea still made a smile tickle the corners of her mouth. How much worse could it really be? She was already a vampire. Would going furry every once in a while be that much of a big deal?

No. But at the same time, she knew it would. She sighed. Why had she ever wished to get rid of the boredom? She certainly wasn't bored anymore. And she had a pretty good suspicion it would be a while before she could claim she was bored again.

"No. I couldn't. That's actually what I came here to talk to you about last night, before things got out of hand." He took a deep breath as if steeling himself for his explanation. "I wanted you the second I saw you. No, it was more than that. I've always been told that I'll know my mate when I see her, but I never believed it until I saw you."

So that was what he thought she was? His mate? She blinked back in surprise. She wasn't even his kind.

"Don't tell me you don't feel it too," he continued, walking closer until he was only inches away. He cupped her face in his palm. "I know you feel something for me that's more than lust. I see it in your eyes whenever you look at me."

Was he stupid? Of course she did. Had for a long time, but she hadn't been willing to admit it. She hadn't even known him properly until a few days ago, and admitting that she wanted him in her life had seemed crazy right up until this moment. It still seemed crazy, but a little less so in light of recent events. "Okay, for the sake of argument, say I do feel a little something. What's going to happen now, anyway?"

"You've been bitten, Joy. I would imagine, since you're technically human, all your reactions will be the same. You'll be able to change."

She wrinkled her nose. He said it like it was some kind of privilege, when she had a feeling it would be a long time before she thought of it as anything more than creepy. "Like at the full moon?"

He laughed, though the expression on his face was still serious. "No. Whenever you want to. Once you've made the change a few times, it'll come easily to you."

"What about you?"

The look he gave her was full of confusion.

"In order for a human to become a vampire, an exchange of blood has to occur. Even a small exchange will do it. You bit me, I bit you. Are you getting the picture yet?"

His eyes widened and he dropped his hand. "Shit."

"My thoughts exactly."

"So where do we go from here?"

She shrugged. "I have no clue. I guess we'll just have to wait and see."

A smile broke out over his face and she couldn't help smiling back. All these weeks of pining for her neighbor, and she'd never imagined it would work out like this. It wasn't what she'd wanted, but now that she had it she couldn't say she was disappointed. All in all, it would prove to be a very interesting life.

EPILOGUE

*N*ATHAN WATCHED JOY STEP out of the darkness and walk toward him. His heart skipped a beat. Two years. It had been two years since fate—and a few little accidents—had brought them together. Now that he had her, he intended to never let her go. There were dozens of women at his brother's engagement party, yet he'd barely noticed any of them.

She reached him and wrapped her arms around his neck, planting a long, wet kiss on his lips before she stepped back and laughed. Her gaze drifted to his brother Tyler and his bride-to-be. "Cute couple."

"Yeah." He put his arm around Joy's shoulder and pulled her closer. "Why didn't we ever have anything like this?"

She rolled her eyes. "Because we're not getting married, silly."

"Want to?"

Her gaze flew to his, her lips parted. It took her a few seconds to answer. "Are you serious?"

"Yep." He'd been thinking about it for a while. A good six months at least. Maybe even longer. She meant everything to him, and he honestly didn't know what had taken him so long to ask. It had just slipped out, but now that he'd said the words he realized he'd been waiting to say them for a long time.

Joy said nothing for so long he thought she might turn him down. But finally, *finally*, she smiled. "That's got to be the most unconventional proposal I've ever heard."

"Is that a yes?"

"Uh-huh. But you have to do something for me first."

"What's that?"

"You have to tell your family."

That was all she wanted? That was an easy request. "My family loves you. In fact, my mom's been bugging me for way too long to pop the question."

"That's not what I'm talking about." She glanced up at him, the look in her eyes nothing short of wicked. "You need to tell them that you're a vampire now too."

He sighed. Yeah, he did need to spill that little secret. He'd planned on keeping it to himself for as long as he could, but if that was what Joy wanted, he'd give it to her. "Okay. But let me do it my own way."

"Thanks, Nathan. I love you, you know."

He leaned down and kissed the top of her head, already planning what he'd say to his mother. No matter what happened, it would end up being an interesting conversation. "I love you too."